*Sarah Morgan is a rising star of
Medical Romance™, and we hope that you'll
enjoy her passionately intense and dramatic
stories in Modern Romance™ too…*

Praise for Sarah Morgan:

'Sarah Morgan [creates] a dynamic
and intense read'
–*Romantic Times*

'Sarah Morgan's likeable characters
will draw you in…'
–*www.romantictimes.com*

THE GREEK TYCOONS

They're the men who have everything—
except a bride…

Wealth, power, charm—what else could a heart-
stoppingly handsome tycoon need?
In THE GREEK TYCOONS mini-series you have
already been introduced to some gorgeous Greek
multimillionaires who are in need of wives.

Now it's time to meet the irresistible Zander Volakis
in Sarah Morgan's

THE GREEK'S BLACKMAILED WIFE

This tycoon has decided it's time
to reclaim his wife…*whatever* it takes!

*Look out for more Greek Tycoons—
coming soon in Modern Romance™!*

THE GREEK'S BLACKMAILED WIFE

BY
SARAH MORGAN

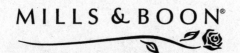

MILLS & BOON®

To the real Lauranne, KLY, for being brilliant in every way.
xxx

First published in Great Britain 2004
Harlequin Mills & Boon Limited,
Eton House, 18-24 Paradise Road, Richmond, Surrey TW9 1SR

© Sarah Morgan 2004

ISBN 0 263 83770 X

Set in Times Roman 10½ on 11¼ pt.
01-0904-52114

Printed and bound in Spain
by Litografia Rosés, S.A., Barcelona

CHAPTER ONE

THE atmosphere in the boardroom crackled with tension, all eyes fixed on the man at the head of the table.

Zander Volakis, Greek billionaire and the object of a million women's fantasies, lounged in his chair with careless ease, the deadly glitter in his eyes the only indication that he'd even heard the heated discussion that had just taken place.

Broad-shouldered and impossibly handsome, his hard jaw was darkened with the beginnings of stubble, evidence of the punishing hours he'd been working to secure this deal.

Waiting for him to deliver his verdict, the men in the room watched him with a mixture of awe and envy while the two women on his board experienced entirely different emotions.

Finally, after what seemed like a million hours to the others, he drew breath.

'I want that island.' His tone deceptively mild, he raked the tense faces of the men and women around the table with night-black eyes. 'So we look for another solution.'

'There is no solution,' someone said bravely. 'People have been trying to buy that island from Theo Kouropoulos for twenty-six years. The guy won't sell.'

Zander sat totally still, his expression veiled by lashes indecently long and thick. 'He's going to sell.'

The board members exchanged furtive glances, each one wondering how to perform the expected miracle.

In the end it was the lawyer who spoke. 'He might sell—' he licked dry lips, fingering the papers in front of him '—if we could change your image.'

The tension around the table increased.

Zander surveyed him steadily, a ghost of a smile playing around his hard mouth. 'My image?'

His lawyer gave a nervous smile. 'Think about who you're dealing with. Theo Kouropoulos has been married to the same woman for fifty years. They have six children and fourteen grandchildren. Family values are high on his agenda and Blue Cove Island is a family resort. As things stand, he doesn't think you're the right buyer.' He drew breath and sat up straighter, bracing himself. 'To quote him exactly, you're "an ice-cold, ruthless businessman with a wicked reputation for womanising and no commitment to family life."'

Zander didn't shift in his seat, the casual lift of a dark eyebrow a clear indication that he failed to see the relevance of his reputation. 'And?'

Alec exchanged a helpless glance with the finance director. 'And the bottom line is that he doesn't want to sell you his family resort. You're the acknowledged leader in creating hotel complexes for singles and couples. You understand what they need for a great holiday. Blue Cove Island is different and it's not like anything you've done before.'

'You argue his case very convincingly,' Zander said smoothly, toying with the pen in front of him. 'Are you working for him or for me?'

Sensitive to the deadly tone behind the softly spoken words, the lawyer flushed but carried on bravely. 'The bottom line is that if you want that island, you need to change your image.' He looked nervously at Zander. 'Or you could think about acquiring a wife.'

An appalled, fascinated silence spread across the spacious glass-walled room. The floor-to-ceiling windows afforded breathtaking views over the heat-soaked, traffic-clogged city of Athens, but no one was looking at the view.

They were all looking at Zander, their gazes uniformly frozen in horrified anticipation as they waited for his reaction.

'I will not,' he declared silkily, 'be acquiring a wife.'

Nervous laughter followed this announcement and Alec cleared his throat again.

'Right. Well, in that case I suggest you see this company I've found.' He shuffled through a pile of papers on his desk. 'They're in London, but you're flying there on business tomorrow for two weeks so we can easily fit a meeting into your schedule. They specialise in public image. Their results are outstanding and they're discreet. I think you should at least talk to them.'

Zander studied him silently, battling with the intense and unwelcome emotions that had been stirred up at the mere mention of matrimony. He had buried those feelings deeply in the darkest corners of his soul and their sudden emergence, as new and fresh as ever, came as an unwelcome shock.

A wife was most certainly *not* a viable solution to his current problem.

Which left the option of changing his image.

He gritted his teeth. The prospect filled him with no small degree of impatience. He'd *never* cared about other people's opinions. Until now. When his reputation was jeopardising the purchase of Blue Cove Island.

Nothing in his expression revealed just how important this deal was to him.

He wanted that island.

He'd wanted it for twenty-six years but he'd been biding his time, waiting for the right moment.

And that moment was now.

'All right.' He stood up with all the grace of a lethal jungle animal, his movements remarkably smooth for such a powerfully built man. 'Let's change my image.'

'So we really know nothing about them? Not even the name of the company?'

Lauranne O'Neill flicked through some slides on her computer, checking her presentation one more time.

'Nothing. They were very cagey.' Mary, her PA, shot her an apologetic look and then cast her eyes over the meeting room one more time. 'Intriguing, isn't it? Maybe they're royalty. The guy I spoke to just said that they wanted to talk to us and that it was highly confidential.'

Lauranne gave a wry smile. 'So confidential that they can't even tell us the company name?'

'I don't care what they're called as long as they pay good money.' Tom, her business partner, strode into the room briskly, a pile of corporate brochures under his arm in readiness. 'They're on their way up. Amanda just went to collect them from Reception.'

Lauranne looked at him with amusement. 'Do you ever think about anything except the bottom line, Tom?'

'No.' He slapped the pile of reports on the table. 'And that's what keeps this company so healthy. You're the conscience—I'm the cash register.'

Lauranne laughed and she was still smiling when Amanda, one of their junior executives, came into the room, her face bright with excitement.

Obviously the client was someone well known and very rich if Amanda's reaction was anything to go by, Lauranne reflected wryly as she smoothed her silk skirt over her slim thighs and pinned a polite smile on her face.

It was a smile that turned to a shocked gasp as she caught her first glimpse of her prospective client.

Zander Volakis.

Staggeringly handsome and arrogantly male, he strolled into the room as if he owned it, closely followed by a team of suited men all keeping a respectful distance behind the boss.

Lauranne stood, welded to the spot, her body frozen. For a moment she thought she might have lost her ability to feel. And then her past exploded into her present and the pain shot through her. Intense, dark pain that should have lessened with time but instead seemed more acute than ever. Pain that ripped away the layers of protection she'd carefully built between her and the world. Pain that had been buried deep for five, long years.

She stared into that cold, handsome face and felt her insides lurch.

He hadn't changed at all.

He was still impossibly good-looking and unashamedly Greek. Sleek dark hair swept back from a smooth, tanned brow, a straight, aristocratic nose, a hard jaw that was almost permanently darkened by stubble and a physique so powerfully masculine that it made women drool.

Intercepting her stunned gaze, those brilliant dark eyes lasered onto hers with all the lethal accuracy of a deadly weapon.

A shiver ran through her trembling body as she read the challenge in that dark gaze.

Zander the hunter.

Pursuing his prey with the same single-minded ruthlessness that he used to outmanoeuvre his competitors. This was a man who had never encountered failure. A man who took millions and turned them into billions.

A man who didn't know the meaning of the word no.

But he was going to have to learn it, she told herself. Because there was absolutely no way she was ever saying yes to this man again.

And there was no way she would give him the satisfaction of seeing just how strongly he affected her.

She lifted her chin and returned his gaze full on. 'Go to hell, Zander.'

There was an audible gasp from the team of people with him but Zander didn't flinch, tension emanating from every inch of his powerful frame as he surveyed her with glittering dark eyes.

'Are you going to make this personal?'

She lifted a hand to her throat, feeling her pulse pounding under the tips of her fingers. 'You bet I am. How can it not be personal?' After everything that had happened between them, *how could it not be personal?* 'You have the sensitivity of an atomic bomb,' she said hoarsely and their gazes locked in combat, neither of them even remotely aware of their audience.

Mary gave a tiny whimper of shock and exchanged horrified glances with Tom, who stood white-faced and silent in one corner of the room.

One of the men with Zander stepped forward, eyeing the two of them cautiously. 'Miss O'Neill? I'm Alec Trevelyan. I'm a lawyer.' The man tried a smile and then gave up, visibly discomforted by the scene playing out around him. 'I work for Volakis Industries.'

'Then I hope you keep your c.v. up to date,' Lauranne said caustically, not even glancing in his direction, 'because working for Volakis Industries is an extremely precarious form of employment.'

The lawyer, mystified and deprived of speech, looked at his boss for some sort of enlightenment. He didn't receive any. Zander Volakis continued to stare at the woman in front of him, nothing in his handsome face giving the slightest clue as to his thoughts.

The lawyer turned back to Lauranne, a pained expression on his face. It was clear he'd never had to deal with this sort of reception before.

He cleared his throat awkwardly. 'You do realise who—?' He gestured to Zander, everything about his body language respectful to the point of being reverential. 'I mean—Zander is—'

'I know *exactly* who he is,' Lauranne said clearly, her wide blue eyes fixed on that breathtakingly handsome face in blatant challenge. 'He's the bastard who tried to ruin my life.' She paused, her breathing as rapid as her heart rate. 'He's also my husband.'

She heard the collective gasp of shock and felt a shaft of pain. The knowledge that he hadn't told them, *that he hadn't even admitted his marriage to her,* wounded her so badly that she wanted to curl up in the corner of the room and hide.

And that was exactly what she'd been doing for the past five years, of course.

Hiding.

Hiding from her past. Hiding from her marriage. Hiding from her feelings.

She lifted her chin, pride giving her strength. 'Did you forget to mention that?' Her eyes were still fixed on Zander, sparking fire and flame. 'How remiss of you. If you wanted it kept a secret then you picked the wrong woman. I'm not prepared to be anyone's dark secret.'

Something flashed in those molten dark eyes. For a fleeting moment she thought it might be admiration but then she shook herself. Zander didn't admire the sort of woman she was. He liked meek, obedient women who played the game and she'd *never* played the game.

She didn't do meek, and she didn't do obedient either.

Alec slid a finger inside his collar, sweat visible on his brow. 'Well, obviously this—er— I mean we didn't— Miss O'Neill— I mean Mrs Volakis—' He broke off and glanced nervously at his boss, waiting for some sort of reaction.

But Zander didn't speak.

He just watched her.

Using silence as the ultimate weapon. *Letting everyone else around him sweat,* Lauranne thought grimly.

She clenched her teeth but she didn't drop her gaze. Wouldn't give him the satisfaction. She knew his tricks. Knew just how skilled he was at manipulating his opponent. If he thought he could intimidate her, then he'd misjudged her.

But then misjudging her was an art that he'd perfected.

'Why are you here?' Her breathing laboured, Lauranne straightened her slim shoulders and at that point Tom cleared his throat and stepped forward.

'This is obviously a mistake. We should just cancel this meeting—'

Still on the receiving end of Zander's cold stare, Lauranne saw the instant change in him. Saw the lethal flash of white-hot anger as he registered Tom's voice. The stillness in that athletic frame fell away to be replaced by a tension so powerful that she took an instinctive step backwards. Connected as she was to that dark, molten gaze, she felt his mood shift from restrained to furious with staggering speed. It was like staring into the crater of a volcano on the very brink of eruption.

He dragged his gaze away from hers and fixed his attention on Tom, his fabulous eyes glittering dangerously, anger visible in every angle of his powerful body.

Transported back five years, Lauranne sucked in a breath.

With the shockingly expensive designer suit and the Rolex watch on his wrist, Zander might *look* every inch the civilised businessman, but she knew that he was anything but civilised. Behind the trappings of success that he wore with such effortless style lurked a male so basic and primitive in his perspective on life that a loincloth would have been more appropriate dress.

'Zander, no—!'

Suddenly she was the one trying to calm things and instinctively she stepped in front of Tom.

'Still protecting him, Lauranne?' Zander's eyes flashed dark, his voice thickened with anger as he whirled on his unsuspecting employees. 'Get out. All of you get out.'

The rest of his team stared at him in blatant shock, horrified and fascinated by this unusual display of emotion from a man renowned for his self-control.

Alec cleared his throat, his consternation evident. 'Zander, maybe we should—'

'I want to talk to *my wife*,' Zander growled, turning back to Lauranne. His gaze slammed into hers with the force of a missile. 'Get rid of Farrer.'

His own team made their retreat so hastily that if the situation hadn't been so serious she would have laughed at how pathetic they were.

But the situation *was* serious, and she wasn't laughing.

Her heart hammering against her chest, Lauranne swallowed and turned to Tom, desperate to defuse a highly charged situation.

'Go,' she urged, her slim fingers closing over the back of a chair for support. Her legs were shaking and her palms were clammy. 'Just go! And you too, Amanda.'

Tom hesitated, both eyes fixed warily on Zander. 'I'm not leaving you with *him*.'

She saw Zander's shoulders tense, saw naked male jealousy and something deeper and far, far more dangerous.

'*Tom*—'

Evidently sensing that danger himself, Tom hurried to the door, following in the wake of Zander's stunned employees.

'Just remember, Lauranne.' Tom stopped by the door, keeping one eye on Zander as if he were a dangerous animal who might attack at any moment. 'Remember what he *did*.'

Zander braced his muscular shoulders. 'You're extremely brave with one hand on the door handle, Farrer.' His tone was lethally soft and Lauranne watched with dismay as the colour drained from Tom's face at the barely veiled threat.

Feeling the tension in the room rise to critical levels, she felt an uncontrollable surge of panic, remembering what had happened last time these two men had confronted each other. *And she'd been the cause of the confrontation.* It was *her* fault that Zander hated Tom. She was *totally* to blame and she'd lived with the guilt ever since—

'Stop it!' Her voice shook and her breath came in unreliable pants. 'Stop it, the pair of you!' Still gripping the chair, her knuckles white, Lauranne glared first at Zander and then at Tom. 'Go! For goodness sake, please *go!* Can't you see that you're just making things worse?'

With a final scowl at Zander, Tom slid out of the room and suddenly they were left alone.

Zander went straight into attack mode, his eyes fierce and his mouth tight with restrained emotion as he launched his first missile. 'You went into business with *him?* With *Farrer?*'

Suddenly she was glad there was a table between them. It prevented her from hurling herself at him and committing bodily harm.

'Yes!' With Tom safely out of the room, she wanted to rub it in. Wanted to poke a stick at the tiger and see just how long it took for him to stop snarling and goad him into action. It was a dangerous game but she couldn't help herself. What right did he have to question her? To stand there with that contemptuous look on his disgustingly handsome face. 'Yes, I did. I went into business with him. Tom was good to me.' She spat the words out and Zander gave a growl and faced her across the table.

'I know exactly how *good* he was to you, Lauranne,' he growled savagely, his voice thick with anger. 'I witnessed it firsthand.'

Her grip tightened on the chair and her breathing jerked. 'We're not going there, Zander. It was five years ago. If you'd wanted to talk we should have done it then but you threw me out. I refuse to discuss it with you now.'

'There was nothing to talk about,' he growled, livid streaks of colour emphasising his intensely masculine bone structure. 'When a Greek man finds his wife in bed with another man, the talking stops.'

He swore in Greek and paced over to the window while Lauranne watched in appalled fascination. She'd never been able to understand how Zander Volakis had gained his reputation for being ice-cold. With her he was so volatile and explosive that he could legitimately be held personally responsible for global warming.

'What are you doing here?' Without the protection of the table between them, Lauranne eyed him with healthy caution, all her senses primed for flight. 'Why have you come here now? It's been five years—'

Five years during which she had tried to come to terms with their brief and totally disastrous marriage. Five years of trying to put each shattered piece of her life back together, hoping that the glue would hold.

Zander didn't turn and her eyes fixed on the back of his neck, on the dark hair that just touched his collar. His hair had always fascinated her. It was the only thing about him that was soft and she knew exactly how it would feel under her fingers. Silky. *Tempting.* So many times she'd slid her hands into that hair, holding his head while he kissed her to the point of meltdown.

Determined not to dwell on his considerable skills in that direction, she dragged her mind back to the present. 'Why did you pick this company?'

He turned then, all forceful virile male, dominating her meeting room with the sheer force of his presence and personality.

'I didn't.'

She gave a humourless laugh as his words registered. 'You didn't know it was me, did you? One of your poor, unsuspecting minions recommended my company and *you didn't know it was me—*'

'But I should have guessed from the name.' He gave a sardonic smile. 'Phoenix PR. Rising from the ashes, Lauranne?'

She glared at him, her cheeks flushed with colour. 'And you created those ashes, Zander,' she reminded him hoarsely, her chest rising and falling as she sucked in air.

'You fired me and made sure I wouldn't get another job. You *ruined* my reputation.'

And he'd trampled on her heart into the bargain but she had too much pride to raise that with him. He'd proved that he didn't care about her and she was damned if she was even going to *hint* at how much she'd cared about him. He was a heartless bastard and she should have had more sense than to become involved with him in the first place.

'Evidently not.' His gaze was ironic as he glanced round the smart meeting room. 'You've done well for yourself.'

It was typical of Zander to judge someone by their business success, she reflected bitterly. Professionally she *had* done well, but as for the other areas of her life—

She wondered what he'd say if he knew that she hadn't been on a date for five years. That every evening she worked until she was exhausted and then just went home and fell into bed. That she was afraid to slow down in case her emotions caught up with her. In case she suddenly started to *feel*.

Emotionally numb and physically exhausted was the only way she could safely exist.

But Zander wasn't interested in emotion. He just didn't *do* emotion.

He'd deleted their brief marriage from his memory with the same ruthless efficiency with which he organised the rest of his life.

Lauranne lifted her chin. Thanks to him, she'd learned not to do emotion either. If he wanted to talk business, then they'd talk business. 'The business is a success thanks to Tom. He financed this business with his own money. He took me on when no other company would touch me.' Her voice shook as she reminded him of the facts. 'If it hadn't been for him I would have had no way of earning a living.'

He rounded on her with a ferocious growl. '*Don't* mention his name in my hearing.'

She felt the hairs stand up on the back of her neck. 'Give me one reason why not.'

His eyes flashed fire and flame. 'Because you were *mine*,' he said thickly, his tone pure masculine possession. '*Mine*. And Farrer did what no other man would have dared to do. Only ignorance could have prompted him into such a foolish and risky course of action.'

Her heart was thudding so hard she thought it must be visible to him. 'He didn't know what sort of man you are.'

'I'm Greek,' he announced flatly. 'And Greek men know how to take care of their women.'

She needed no reminder of his heritage. It was part of who he was, visible in everything he did and everything he said.

'Your relationship with women is stuck in the Stone Age. If Versace made loincloths you'd be wearing one.'

'I didn't notice you complaining when you were naked under me.' His voice was a rich, masculine drawl and she felt it curl its way around every part of her damaged and fragile heart. The vision of lying naked with him was all too clear and she felt an unwelcome coil of heat low in her pelvis.

The discovery that part of her still craved him came as an unpleasant shock.

She lifted her chin, struggling to hang onto her dignity. 'I'd like you to leave right away.'

'Because you don't trust yourself around me, Lauranne?'

'Because I'm afraid I might bruise you if you stay within thumping distance,' she said grittily. 'Fighting always was what we did best.'

He lifted an eyebrow mockingly, back in control once again. 'That's not how I remember it, *agape mou*. We did a lot of things extremely well.'

Their eyes clashed and she caught her breath, remembering, feeling—

Oh, God, she didn't want to feel…

'Go, Zander. Just go.'

But he didn't go. Instead he strolled towards her, his eyes still locked with hers in blatant challenge.

She forced herself to hold her ground. Forced herself not to turn and run despite the quivering of her body and the lurch of her heart.

'You always reminded me of a firework,' he murmured, his tone conversational as he steadily closed the distance between them. 'Sparky, full of fire and beautiful enough to make a man gasp. And dangerous to handle.'

His words made her breathing jerk. 'Come any closer and you're going to find out just how dangerous. And stop pretending that we had any sort of relationship that meant anything. To you it was just sex and you were only interested in me because I refused you.'

'Not true,' he shot back instantly. 'I was interested because you challenged me. With every flash of your blue eyes and every lift of that delicate chin, you challenged me.' He came to a halt directly in front of her, a smile playing around his firm mouth. 'But it's true that no woman had ever run away from me before. It was a first.'

'You are impossibly arrogant.' She gave an exclamation of disgust and his smile widened.

'I'm honest. And we both know that you were just playing games. You were mine from the moment I saw you sitting on that bar stool, that tiny skirt showing every inch of your fabulous long legs, your golden hair trailing down your back like a beacon lighting up the night sky.'

Her pulse was fluttering and she shook her head in denial. 'I *never* would even have spoken to you if I'd known who you were.'

He lifted a hand and touched her hair with gentle fingers, his touch making her tremble.

'You couldn't help yourself, Lauranne. And neither could I. It was stronger than both of us—'

And it was still stronger than both of them.

This close she was aware of every single inch of him. She could see the strong column of his throat, smell the tantalising male smell that she associated only with Zander, and she could feel the power of his sexuality with every traitorous bone in her body. He was just so wickedly attractive, she thought desperately, remembering the way he'd murmured huskily to her in Greek as he'd rolled her under him on a warm sandy beach.

She pushed the thought away, wondering why the brain remembered good when there was so much bad to choose from.

'If I'd known who you were I would have known you were trouble. Your reputation alone would have made me run a mile.'

Dear God, how could she feel like this? Even after everything he'd done to her, she could feel the heat of desire burning inside her, the incessant throb of the blood in her veins.

It was as if her body were suddenly coming to life after five years of hibernation.

Only Zander had ever done this to her.

Only Zander drove her to a pitch of sexual excitement that eclipsed the workings of her brain.

And he hadn't even touched her—

He was dangerous, deadly and thoroughly addictive.

'You were a fascinating mixture of sparky and shy,' he observed, totally ignoring her snappy response. 'Nervous of me but excited and intrigued at the same time.'

Suddenly it was difficult to speak. 'I was right to be nervous of you. I should have run a mile.'

'Instead of which you married me.'

His cool statement sucked the breath from her lungs. Yes, she'd married him. Because she'd been so madly, crazily in love with him that from the day she'd met him the only word in her vocabulary had been 'yes.'

'Everyone makes mistakes, Zander.' And she was still

paying for hers. Every minute of every day. 'You're ruthless and cold-hearted and I truly don't believe that you have a compassionate bone in your body.'

He stared at her for a long moment, a muscle working in his lean jaw. 'There are plenty of people out there who would agree with you,' he drawled, 'which brings us back to the reason I'm here.'

Her brain did an emergency stop. She'd actually forgotten that there must be a reason for his visit.

'You're here because your people made a big mistake,' she reminded him caustically. 'You wouldn't have come if you'd known it was me. And now you know, you can leave the same way you came in.'

'I don't think so.' There was a strange light in his eyes. 'You see, after five years I've finally found a use for you. You're going to work for me again.'

CHAPTER TWO

LAURANNE stared at Zander in stunned silence.

He wanted her to work for him?

Was he mad?

Had he forgotten everything that had happened between them?

Had he forgotten the hideous details?

Her skin prickled and she suddenly felt hot. Terribly hot. 'You must be joking. I will *never* work for you again.'

A smooth dark eyebrow lifted and he smiled, totally unperturbed by her passionate declaration. 'You think not?'

She stared at him helplessly, realising too late that she'd said the wrong thing. A blatant refusal simply fuelled his ferociously competitive instinct. No one *ever* refused Zander Volakis anything. It just cemented his desire to win.

He was assuming she'd issued him a challenge, instead of which her refusal to work for him had originated from the most basic instinct for survival.

She resisted the impulse to slap the arrogant smile from his handsome face. 'This isn't one of your games, Zander. I wish you'd never come here but seeing as you have we might as well sort things out once and for all.' Her heart was banging against her ribs as she came to an instant decision. 'I—I want a divorce.'

There was a pulsing silence and he surveyed her with a maddening degree of cool.

'You want a divorce?' He sounded faintly amused. 'This is very sudden, *agape mou.* After five years you suddenly want a divorce?'

Five years of utter misery. Five years of burying her past

21

and trying to get on with her life. It was like ignoring an enormous wound and hoping that it would heal by itself.

But it hadn't healed. Maybe a divorce was the answer.

'We made a mistake, Zander,' she croaked, wishing her insides didn't feel so raw. 'Let's put it right.'

Then maybe she could finally let go and get on with her life.

There was a long silence and Zander watched her thoughtfully. 'All right,' he said finally. 'Do this job for me, and I'll consider it.'

'No!' She didn't want him to turn it into one of his deals. She just wanted him to leave before she fell apart. 'I don't want to work for you again.'

It was just too painful. Seeing him again.

Being this close—

He paced slowly across the carpet, infuriatingly calm in the face of her growing anger. 'You're running a business, Lauranne. Can you afford to turn away wealthy clients?'

'Whatever you offered would never be enough to even vaguely tempt me to work for you again,' she said bitterly. 'There's more to a business than money.'

He laughed. 'If you think that then it's a wonder you're still trading.'

'Well, I wouldn't expect you to understand what I mean,' she flung back, her eyes blazing with the fire of past injuries. 'You only ever look at the bottom line.'

'Where else is there to look?'

'At people! People matter, Zander. People have feelings—' She broke off, horrified with herself for becoming so emotional. How could it still hurt so much? Whoever said that time heals had never been in love with Zander Volakis. She was rapidly discovering that time hadn't healed anything at all. Trying to calm herself, she reached out and poured herself a glass of water with a shaking hand. 'Believe it or not, when I refused to see you I was not issuing you with a challenge.' *She'd been protecting herself.* 'I don't want to have anything to do with you and I can't think why you would want me to work for you again.'

'Because I need someone to do a good job.'

Her fingers tightened around the glass and she glared at him, hating him for coming back into her life. Hating herself for reacting so strongly. 'And what makes you think I'd do a good job for you?'

'Three reasons come to mind,' he drawled lazily. 'Firstly because I will pay you an indecent sum of money that you can't afford to turn down; secondly because if you don't do a good job, then I won't give you that divorce that you suddenly seem to want so much.'

Lauranne licked dry lips. 'You said three reasons.' Her voice was little more than a croak. 'What's the third?'

He smiled. 'Thirdly you will do the very best job you can, because if you mess up then I'll ruin you and I'll ruin Farrer.' He gave a casual shrug. 'Simple really.'

The glass slid from her hand and shattered on the floor. Like my life, Lauranne thought numbly, not even bothering to pick up the pieces as she stared at Zander. 'You can't be serious.'

'I never joke about work,' he said smoothly. 'You should know that much about me.'

She did know. When it came to work, Zander was single-minded. Driven.

She tried another tack. 'You can't possibly want me to work for you again. Not after everything that happened.'

'Five years ago I wasn't safe to be in the same room as you,' he agreed, 'but thankfully I've moved on since then. You'll work for me, Lauranne.' He delivered his statement with cool confidence, his total lack of emotion in direct contrast to her own highly charged feelings. His careless, arrogant assumption that she'd eventually agree to his demands increased the tension in the room by dramatic degrees.

'You fired me,' she said, her voice shaking with a passion

so powerful that it threatened to consume her usually rational self. 'You fired me publicly and then ruined my reputation so thoroughly that no other company would touch me.'

He shrugged, casually dismissive of her passionate statement. 'What happened between us is in the past. Fortunately for you, I'm willing to forget what you did.'

She gaped at him, rendered speechless by his overwhelming arrogance.

Forget?

Had their marriage really affected him so little that he could forget?

And did he really think that *she* would ever forget?

Had he really no idea just what he'd done to her? How much she'd suffered because of him? Part of her was proud that she'd survived in spite of him and part of her wanted to leap on him and claw at that devastatingly handsome face if only to provoke some degree of emotional response.

'You're my husband and yet you tried to destroy me.' Her voice was little more than a whisper. 'You took vows, Zander. Made promises. And none of them meant anything to you, did they? You are utterly ruthless and I will remind myself of that fact every single day of my life.'

Black eyes clashed with blue. 'You angered me.'

Such a simple statement with which to justify brutal behaviour. He was just *so* Greek, she reflected helplessly, his otherwise razor-sharp intellect neutralised by his driving need for revenge.

He stepped towards her and she tensed, her body rendered immobile by the naked sexuality in his masculine gaze. She felt that gaze with every feminine part of her quivering body. Heat built inside her and slowly spread outwards, consuming her with its intensity. Her knees wobbled and she was forced to face the inevitable. That even hating him she still wanted him with every fibre of her being.

How could she?

How could her body still react to the man when her mind was ordering her to feel nothing and run?

But it was impossible to stand this close to Zander Volakis and feel nothing. She was still helplessly vulnerable to his overwhelming sexuality.

Appalled by that revelation, she reminded herself that she might not be able to control her reaction to him, but she could certainly control her actions and she had more sense than to act on those feelings.

Determined to conquer her own weakness, Lauranne curled her fingers into her palms. 'Get out before I call Security.'

The faint lift of his brow and the hint of amusement in his dark eyes drew attention to the foolishness of her words. Her 'Security' consisted of the caretaker who maintained the building and was nominally responsible for keeping the alarm system in working order. Hardly a match for a professional security team, or even Zander himself. He was taller and broader than every other male of her acquaintance and she knew from experience that he was a man who could handle himself physically.

'I think we both know that your ''Security'' are unlikely to challenge me.' Zander moved closer still and suddenly the room seemed airless. The meeting room was huge and light and yet he managed to dominate every inch of the space around him.

'I want you to go. I mean it, Zander.' She dragged her gaze away from those indecently thick dark lashes, trying hard to ignore the masculine jaw and the wide, sensual mouth that could kiss a woman to a state of madness. Instead she forced herself to focus on the pain and the hurt. The destruction of her life. The man was a ruthless hunter. He took what he wanted and then moved on, stepping neatly over the debris that he'd created. 'I have absolutely nothing to say to you. If you truly want to work with my company then you can talk to Tom.'

It was the wrong thing to say.

With appalled fascination she stood totally still, watching the change in him again, seeing the way his broad shoulders tensed in preparation for a fight.

'You have the *nerve* to suggest that I talk to *him,* knowing what I would do to him if he set just one foot inside this office again—are you really that stupid?'

She stared at him, transfixed, hardly daring to move or speak in case her actions inflamed him further.

No. She wasn't stupid.

She'd just forgotten what it was like to deal with an elemental Greek male. All the other men she knew were civilised and mild mannered. Not Zander. He was shockingly primitive, his emotions so hazardous and unpredictable that he should have had 'handle with care' printed on his back.

But she wasn't twenty-one any more and she wasn't going to allow him to intimidate her. 'You don't frighten me, Zander. And if you lay one finger on Tom ever again, I'll— I'll—' She broke off, helplessly, aware of just how ridiculous her threats must seem to this man.

'You'll what?' Dark eyes clashed with hers, his gaze heavily loaded with derision. 'Still fighting battles for that pathetic little coward, Lauranne?'

'He isn't pathetic—'

'He left you in here with me,' Zander pointed out dryly, his tone dripping with masculine derision. 'Hardly the actions of a hero, given our past history. He should have been in here, protecting his woman.'

'I was *never* his woman.'

There.

She'd said it. Finally she'd said it. The words she should have spoken five years earlier and would have done if it hadn't been for her stupid pride and a misguided desire to play him at his own game.

But her statement had no impact on Zander. It was five years too late.

'*Don't* insult my intelligence,' he ground out, anger and tension evident in the aggressive thrust of his jaw and the set of his wide shoulders. 'You were in bed with him. And you were wearing my wedding ring at the time.'

Lauranne stared at him helplessly, her chest rising and falling as she struggled to breathe. Zander was Greek to the very backbone and she knew that there was no point in trying to tell him the truth. And anyway, wasn't part of it her fault? Hadn't she manipulated the situation because she'd *wanted* Zander to be jealous? Wanted to punish him for the hurt he'd caused her. And she'd succeeded.

She'd succeeded so well that his reaction had frightened her—

The whole situation had escalated out of control so fast that she hadn't even had a chance to confess the truth. That the embrace he'd witnessed had started off as comfort. A brotherly hug to ease the pain of having discovered that Zander had no intention of changing his playboy lifestyle just because he'd married her.

'It's too late for excuses and explanations,' Zander interrupted harshly. 'You're only making them because you're afraid that I'm not safe around your lover. And you're right. I'm not safe.' His dark eyes glittered dangerously and he fixed his gaze on her face with a fierce intensity. 'I'm not safe at all.'

'Zander—'

'Despite your mouth and your attitude, you were a virgin when I met you.' His tone was raw, his breathing shallow and decidedly unsteady as he wrestled for control. 'So what was it, Lauranne? What happened? Did you need to experiment? Did you need to find out what it was like with other men?'

The injustice of it bit through to her soul.

Her temper flaring, she glared at him. 'You don't have the monopoly on variety, Zander.'

It was a foolish, inflammatory thing to say and the mo-

ment the words left her mouth she wished she could re-
tract them.

Zander Volakis was a poor choice of adversary.

His eyes clashed with hers and Lauranne felt like an animal caught in headlights, aware of the rapid approach of
danger but unable to move. Instinctively she tensed and prepared for impact. She heard his sharply indrawn breath, saw
the flash of anger in his eyes and knew she was looking at
a man at the very edge of tolerance.

His mouth was pressed together in a grim line, his gaze
hostile and challenging, and she realised that the past was
a subject she was never going to be able to discuss with this
man unless he was physically restrained. He just wouldn't
listen to her. Not then and not now.

It was only when he unexpectedly turned and started
scanning the photographs and award certificates on the walls
that she suddenly realised that she'd been holding her
breath.

Starved of oxygen, her head thumping and her heart banging against her chest, Lauranne dragged some much-needed
air into her lungs. Forcing herself to breathe slowly she
glanced around her. She couldn't run because he could out-
run her, so all she could do was wait, unsure as to when
the next attack would come.

He stopped in front of one of her certificates, legs planted
firmly apart in an attitude of pure male dominance. 'You've
received plenty of awards—'

'I'm good at my job. And I was good at my job when
you fired me.'

He ignored that. 'We'd gone way past a business relationship.'

And that had been her biggest mistake, of course.

She'd married the boss. And when her marriage had fallen
apart, so had her career.

'You were my wife and you betrayed me,' he growled.

'And now you have what you obviously wanted. A new life with your lover.'

Lauranne gaped at him, deprived of speech by his spectacular misinterpretation of the facts.

'Tom is *not* my lover.'

If she hadn't been so appalled she would have laughed. This was a man with a brilliant brain, a man whose ability with figures was legendary and who had an awesome reputation for strategic thinking.

Why was it that with her he developed tunnel vision?

How had he added two and two and made fifty?

Hadn't he known how much she'd loved him?

She opened her mouth to ask him that exact question and then closed it again. What was the point? It was too late. Too late for both of them. They'd moved past the point where communication could make a difference. And the past was history now. She just wanted him to be history too and the less she spoke, the better. There was only one level on which they'd ever communicated effectively and she didn't even want to *think* about that.

So she stayed silent, trying to anticipate his next move.

'I don't want Farrer anywhere near my business,' he said harshly, 'but I want you working for me again.'

His emphatic statement should have stimulated a sharp retort on her part but her brain had ceased to function. She was operating on a much baser level.

Mesmerised by his shockingly potent masculinity, Lauranne opened her mouth and her tongue flickered out to moisten her lips. His dark gaze homed in on the gesture with the speed of a heat-seeking missile and suddenly she was holding her breath. *Remembering.*

His eyes lifted back to hers and she felt the tension throb between them, the atmosphere so taut that it threatened to snap at any moment. His eyes dropped to the tiny pulse in her neck and then moved lower still, resting on the soft swell of her breasts under the cream silk blouse.

Did he know?

Did he know what effect he had on her? Fighting the temptation to lift her hands and cover herself, Lauranne stood still, helpless to prevent the hardening of her nipples and the growing ache in her pelvis.

Imprisoned by that shimmering dark gaze, she felt herself melt inside, hypnotised by a force too powerful to resist.

Sexual awareness throbbed between them and then he swore softly in Greek and dragged his gaze away from her, a muscle working in his lean, bronzed cheek.

Of course he knew, she thought helplessly. Hadn't he always known? He'd recognised her response to him before she had. And that was hardly surprising. A man as experienced with her sex as Zander knew everything there was to know about female reactions. He was able to detect the most subtle of signs and know exactly when to make his move.

'Farrer would never be able to satisfy a woman like you.' His harsh statement took her by surprise and she gaped at him, stunned by his unspoken implication that he would be the only male to ever fulfil that task. 'You'd trample all over him.'

'Not every woman is vulnerable to your particular brand of Neanderthal machismo,' she said bitterly and then wished she hadn't because he was across the room in less than two strides, pulling her against him in a powerful movement that reminded her that she was talking utter rubbish.

She was extremely vulnerable and she always had been where Zander was concerned.

'Let's test that theory, shall we?' His dark eyes shielded by impossibly long lashes, he gazed down at her, muttered something in Greek and then brought his mouth down on hers in a kiss of such savage urgency that she had no time even to whimper a protest.

Her mouth opened under the determined pressure of his and then she was kissing him back, her tongue tangling with his, her hands sneaking upwards to lock in his silky black hair.

It was wild and hot, the kiss of a man seeking to stake his claim, and she responded in full measure, her hips grinding against his in an effort to draw herself closer to the very centre of his masculinity.

How she'd missed this—

How she'd missed *him*.

It was as if their bodies recognised each other, drawn together by a force more powerful than the mere physical. She felt him shudder and then he was lifting her onto the desk, curling her legs around his muscular length so that they were held together in the most intimate way possible.

'Not vulnerable?' He growled the words against her mouth and yanked her closer so that she felt the hard throb of his erection against her most sensitive flesh. *'Does he make you feel this, Lauranne?'*

Heat exploded in her pelvis and she squirmed closer still, frustrated by the barriers that still remained.

And then suddenly he released her, uttered a savage curse and extracted himself from the coil of her body with decisive force, leaving her to clutch dizzily at the desk for support.

Her whole body throbbed with a sexual need that she hadn't felt for five long years and for a second she stared at him blankly, unable to comprehend why he had ended something so utterly perfect. Then her passion-clouded brain flickered slowly to life and humiliation set in.

He'd ended it because the kiss had had nothing to do with chemistry and everything to do with revenge. She'd dented his ego and he was punishing her.

What was she doing?

This man was her enemy. Without thinking she'd issued another challenge, this time to his sexuality, and he'd responded by kissing her in anger, using passion as a punishment, not a seduction. The moment his mouth had crushed hers she'd been clinging to him, swept away by a primitive sexual need that she'd only ever felt with this man.

Was she really that shallow?

'I hate you,' she whispered, but the words were meaningless even to her because the lips that formed them were soft and swollen from his kisses and the eyes that glared at him were still hazy with passion.

'I don't care.' He stepped away from her with all the grim satisfaction of a male who had very definitely proved his point. 'I'll pick you up at seven-thirty. We'll discuss terms over dinner.'

Dinner?

She stared at him, muted by the shivers that still affected her body.

'What?' He lifted a smooth, dark eyebrow in her direction. 'No smart remark? No refusal? No, you're the last man on earth I'd eat dinner with? This isn't going to be much fun if you're so compliant, *agape mou.*'

'Why d-dinner?' Still shocked by the intensity of her response to him, her brain seemed to have slowed to a virtual halt.

He dealt her a wry smile. 'Despite the fact you claim not to be vulnerable to me, I suspect that the only way you and I will ever be able to conduct a conversation of any length, *agape mou,* is if we meet in a *very* public place. Hopefully the presence of an audience will curb our natural instincts to strip each other naked.'

She stared at him, shattered at being confronted with such an unpalatable truth. How could she have responded like that? She should have slapped his handsome face, instead of which—

'I have absolutely no trouble resisting you,' she croaked and he smiled.

'Of course you don't.'

His eyes dropped to her breasts and she was suddenly

painfully conscious that her nipples were pushing against the thin fabric of her blouse, visible evidence of her arousal.

Resisting the temptation to cover herself, she lifted her chin, trying to salvage a trace of dignity from the wreckage of her pride.

'I don't want to discuss terms.' She wasn't going to let him threaten her. 'I have nothing to say to you, Zander, in private or in public.'

'Then I'll do the talking.' Totally indifferent to her protests, he strolled casually towards the door and then paused, a hint of danger in his glittering dark eyes as he focused his attention on her one more time. 'Oh, and a word of warning—' his voice was quiet but she tensed, detecting the steel under that deceptively soft tone '—if you want to have a civilised evening, then don't mention Farrer.'

Civilised?

She almost laughed.

How could an evening with Zander ever be civilised? He was the least civilised person she'd ever met.

'I won't be mentioning anything because I'm not meeting you.'

Black eyes slammed into hers, holding her captive. Like two fighters in a ring they faced each other, the atmosphere antagonistic and highly charged.

'Don't play games with me, Lauranne,' he warned softly. 'The stakes are high. Seven-thirty. And you know well enough that if you're not here, I'll find you.'

With that he turned and strolled out of the room with the same degree of cool authority with which he'd entered it.

Lauranne stared after him with helpless hostility, unsure whether to scream or cry. For five years she'd successfully locked her past away. She'd managed to get on with her life. And then Zander had sauntered back into it with his hot black eyes and his arrogant ways and all her attempts to forget what they'd shared, *their marriage,* were ground to dust. One frantic, febrile kiss later and suddenly her emotions were free again.

When he'd walked through the door she'd been spitting and angry, in fact all the things she should have been five years before when she'd been too distraught to defend herself from his accusations.

She knew now what he was and who he was—

Knew that Zander Volakis didn't possess a soft side—

But all that had ceased to matter when he'd kissed her. She'd forgotten everything except the burning heat of his mouth, the erotic probe of his tongue and the hardness of his body against hers. And her traitorous, yearning body had responded with a desperation that had been humiliatingly obvious to a man as experienced and sophisticated as Zander.

She slid off the table and straightened her clothes, wishing that her emotions could be tidied with the same ease. The knowledge that he could still have such a powerful effect on her filled her with despair.

It didn't really matter if he agreed to a divorce, she thought helplessly. What they shared was so powerful that all the lawyers in the world wouldn't be able to negotiate an end to it. And the only answer was to stay away from him.

Once he discovered that he couldn't bully her, he'd leave her alone. He couldn't really ruin the business, she reasoned, mentally running through their list of clients. He was calling her bluff.

Trying to frighten her into submission.

There was no way she was eating dinner with him. In fact there was no way she was going to see him again in any shape or form.

He might be arriving to collect her at seven-thirty, but she wouldn't be here. And if she knew him well enough to know that he'd find her, then *he* should also know *her* well enough to know that she wouldn't make it easy for him.

If he thought he was going to knock on the door and collect her, then he was in for a long and disappointing evening.

CHAPTER THREE

ZANDER strode out to his sports car, furious with himself and cursing his utter lack of control.

What the *hell* had come over him? he wondered savagely as he tossed the file on Phoenix PR onto the passenger seat and slid into the car, oblivious to the rest of his team and his bodyguards who immediately swarmed into the car parked behind. He'd virtually jumped her on her table and he *never* behaved like that. He was a man who prided himself on his self-discipline, on being able to operate without allowing emotions to interfere with his decision-making.

But Lauranne reduced his behaviour to a level so basic that he barely recognised himself.

He'd wanted to punish her—

It had been the shock of seeing her, he reassured himself grimly. He hadn't expected to see her. And he certainly hadn't expected to see Farrer.

It had been the desire to wipe Farrer's name from her lips that had driven him to behave like that, staking a claim where none lay.

And the moment he'd felt her soft mouth open under his he'd been lost, overwhelmed by a raw physical need that he'd never experienced around any woman except Lauranne O'Neill.

Lauranne—

The biggest mistake of his life.

As if to taunt him, a powerful vision exploded inside his brain. A vision of honey-blonde hair and a soft mouth curved in a tempting smile designed to drive a man to the edge of sanity.

36

Lauranne, with her micro miniskirts, endless brown legs and hotly passionate nature.

Zander gave a humourless laugh. For most of his life he'd watched his father make an utter fool of himself over a string of women and he'd vowed *never* to do the same thing himself. There was no way he was ever going to get married. He wasn't so stupid.

But then he'd met Lauranne—

He groaned and leaned his head against the seat of the car, almost able to feel the touch of her mouth on his. From the moment they'd met they'd been enveloped by a scorching fire of passion so intense and primitive that for a short while it had consumed both of them. To the extent that he'd done the one thing he'd always promised himself he'd never do.

He'd married her.

And to this day he didn't understand why he'd done it.

Breathing heavily, Zander reached out a lean brown hand and flipped open the file that his lawyer had given him, his heart thudding as he gazed at the photograph on the first page.

Had he bothered to open the file sooner he might not now be suffering from a severe case of mental and sexual frustration, he reflected grimly, reminding himself to *always* check out every company that his lawyer suggested in future. Had he known it was *her* he would never have agreed to meet her.

Or would he?

Staring down at those amazing blue eyes, he felt a reaction so raw, so primitively sexual that his body stirred in the most masculine way possible. His mouth tightened in bitter self-condemnation. It had always been like that with this woman. From the first moment he'd seen her, sipping a cocktail in one of his bars by the beach, swinging one long tanned leg from the bar stool, he'd been hooked. His reputation for being cool had certainly not been earned on that occasion, he reflected with grim amusement. In fact he'd been so hot for her he'd used every technique in his armoury to ensure that she ended up where he wanted her.

In his bed.

His entire relationship with Lauranne had been one long burn of emotion. He'd brought out the hotly sexual side of her nature and somehow she'd found his sensitive side. Until then he hadn't even known he *had* a sensitive side, but Lauranne had wriggled herself into places previously off limits to all females, no matter how beautiful or satisfying in bed.

Zander studied the cool, businesslike photograph of the woman that he'd once known in the most intimate way that a man could know a woman.

He'd been her first lover and that had given him a satisfaction that only a very traditional Greek male could ever truly understand.

She'd been *his*.

He'd held her as she'd trembled against him, swallowed her cries of ecstasy as he'd introduced her to the pleasures of sex for the first time in her life.

And he'd been ruthlessly unforgiving when he'd discovered her infidelity. His father's experience of women should have more than prepared him for her betrayal, but the emotions he'd experienced had been so powerful that they'd shocked him. He'd felt out of control and he'd *hated* that feeling. He'd just wanted her out of his life before he was tempted to do something even more stupid than marrying her.

Like forgiving her.

His mouth tightened slightly as he scanned the rest of the file, taking in her astonishing achievements in the five years since he'd last seen her. Even as the anger simmered inside him, he found himself admiring the way she'd obviously managed to build a successful business from the ashes of the career that he'd personally destroyed.

But that didn't surprise him. She possessed rare qualities, qualities that he'd spotted within moments of meeting her.

Everything about Lauranne was bright. Her mind, her wit and her shiny blonde hair that had wrapped itself around him in a silken seduction every time they'd made love.

Being with Lauranne had been like gazing into the sun. It had left him blinded and dazzled.

And now she wanted a divorce.

His jaw tightened. He'd never even *thought* about divorce before she'd mentioned it. He'd just put the whole disastrous episode out of his head and got on with his life.

Intensely irritated by the depth of emotion that the mere memory of Lauranne could evoke, Zander snapped the file shut, his eyes suddenly hard.

Swearing fluently in Greek, he pulled into the flow of traffic and made for his office. He needed a cold shower. A very, very cold shower. And after that maybe he'd be able to disengage his libido and engage his brain.

'I couldn't believe it when he walked into the room.' Tom stared at Lauranne in utter dismay. 'Tell me you threw him out.'

She gave a wan smile, thinking of Zander's six-foot-three, muscle-packed frame. 'Hardly.'

Tom paced backwards and forwards in front of her desk. 'I need a cigarette.'

'You gave up six months ago,' Lauranne pointed out gently and he grimaced.

'If Volakis is back in our lives then I'll be taking it up again pretty damn fast.' Tom's face was white. 'And tell me that the two of you are not still married and that you were just playing one of your games. You almost gave me a heart attack when you said "he's my husband" in that chilly tone.'

Lauranne closed her eyes briefly and curled her fingers into her palms. 'We weren't playing games.'

Tom stilled and then shook his head slowly, looking at her in horrified disbelief. 'Oh, no—no, no, no. You're not telling me you *are* still married—'

Lauranne swallowed and nodded.

'Surely you divorced him?' Tom's tone was utterly incredulous and Lauranne bit her lip.

'I didn't get round to it.'

'You didn't get round to it?' Tom gaped at her. 'Why the hell not?'

Because she'd meant every one of her vows. Because divorcing him would have meant facing up to the end of their relationship and she just wasn't able to do that.

'Because I didn't really want to think about it.'

Tom shook his head. 'And Volakis? What's his excuse?'

Lauranne bit her lip. 'I think he probably forgot he was ever married to me,' she croaked and Tom rolled his eyes.

'Oh, great. So technically you're still married to him.' He let out a long breath. 'So what did he want? Apart from causing mayhem, which is his favourite pastime, I seem to recall.'

Lauranne folded her hands in her lap to hide how badly they were shaking. 'He wants me to work for him.'

Tom gave a short disbelieving laugh. 'You're kidding.'

'I wish I was.'

Tom's mouth tightened. 'But you're not going to, right? Tell me you're not even considering it!' He raked his fingers through his already-tumbled blond hair and looked at Lauranne with naked exasperation. 'This is the man who took your heart and trampled it into the dirt, remember? This is the man who slept with another woman, fired you from a job you adored and then did everything in his power to make sure that you couldn't get another one.'

Faced with the unpalatable truth, Lauranne bit her lip. 'I know that, and I'm not—'

'Yes, you are.' Tom let out a frustrated sigh and shook his head in despair. 'I know you *so* well and I know how you felt about him. I also know that there's been no man in your life for the five years since he dumped you. And I'm beginning to question the real reason that you didn't get round to divorcing him.'

'Tom—'

'You're already dreaming about him, aren't you?'

Lauranne opened her mouth, wanting to deny it, but no sound came out.

Tom groaned. 'Don't go getting ideas, Lauranne. Zander Volakis is bad news. He might have just walked back into your life but sooner or later he's going to walk straight back out again, taking all the vulnerable bits of you with him.'

She flinched. 'I know that and I wouldn't—'

'Yes, you would,' Tom said flatly. 'You can't help yourself, and neither can he. It's like watching a natural disaster in the making. Tell me he didn't kiss you.'

She felt betraying colour flood into her cheeks and Tom swore softly.

'I knew it!' He spread his hands in a gesture of exasperation. 'The pair of you can't be in a room and not rip each other's clothes off!'

'Tom, please—'

'Let's get one thing straight.' He pointed a finger at her, stabbing the air to emphasise his point. 'I'm not doing it again! I'm not watching you go through it again, Lauranne. For six months you were an emotional wreck. I had to drag you out of that bed of yours every morning. I'm your best friend, Lauranne, but the guy almost destroyed you. I put you back together piece by piece. I can't do that a second time.'

'I'm not asking you to.' Her voice was little more than a croak as she was forced to face memories that she'd tried to lock safely away. 'I didn't ask him to come here. He just barged in and took over—'

'Conquering Greek tycoon,' Tom said bitterly, pacing

across the office and thumping a fist against the wall. 'You should have told him to go to hell.'

'I tried that, remember? His listening skills definitely need attention.' Lauranne made a pathetic attempt at humour but it fell flat.

'Divorce him, Lauranne. You've got any number of options. Unreasonable behaviour—*adultery*—' Tom's mouth tightened. 'Or had you forgotten the adultery?'

Lauranne felt a lump build in her throat and shook her head. Of course she hadn't forgotten the adultery. Until that awful day she'd never known the true meaning of pain.

Tom sighed. 'So now what? Presumably it was him I saw just now burning up the road in his flash car. Is he coming back?'

Lauranne hesitated. 'He's picking me up at seven-thirty to discuss business over dinner.'

'Dinner?' Tom gaped at her incredulously. 'The last time we saw the guy, you were his dinner and so was I! Main course and dessert. He's a predator, Lauranne, and if you trust him then you're a fool.'

'I don't trust him.'

Tom glared at her. 'This is the man who landed me in hospital—'

She closed her eyes briefly and shivered at the memory. She'd been so afraid. Afraid of what she'd caused. *If she hadn't kissed Tom—* 'I know that, but he's Greek and he saw you and I together and he's a possessive guy—' She broke off, wondering why she was trying to excuse his behaviour.

Judging from the appalled expression on his face, Tom was obviously wondering the same thing. '*Possessive?* Unhinged, you mean. Does being Greek somehow make you lose your brain?' His voice was bitter. 'The guy is supposed to be ferociously intelligent. If he'd looked closely he would have noticed that you'd been howling. Generally speaking when I'm with a woman I don't make her howl.'

Lauranne bit her lip. 'B-but he saw me on the bed with you.'

Tom had the grace to look sheepish. 'Yes—well—' he shrugged awkwardly '—I admit that bit was my fault. I'd been drinking with clients and then you turned up looking all vulnerable and—well—'

'It's all right.' Lauranne reached out a hand and touched his arm. 'We both know it was just the drink that made you leap on me. Just friends, that's all you and I have ever been, isn't it?'

Tom sighed. 'I learned a long time ago that there's only one man on this planet that you ever notice,' he said dryly, 'so fortunately I gave up on you years ago and found myself a decent love life somewhere else.'

Lauranne gave a wan smile. 'Glad one of us did.' Her smile faded. 'It's all my fault that Zander hates you. That night when he found us together— I could have punched you on the nose if I'd wanted to but when I looked up and saw Zander standing there all I could think about was revenge. It was my fault really. I shouldn't have done it. I shouldn't have made him jealous.'

She'd played a dangerous game but she hadn't been thinking straight. In fact she'd discovered that she was capable of being every bit as stubborn and jealous as Zander.

Tom shuddered at the memory. 'Well, do us all a favour and don't make the guy jealous again. Did you see the look on his face when he saw me today? I thought I was dead.'

Before Lauranne could answer Mary came hurrying into the room, pink-cheeked and breathless.

'That was Zander Volakis! The Greek wonder boy— here—in our office—and you, you—' she looked at Lauranne, wide eyed. 'You're *married* to him?'

'In name only,' Lauranne said stiffly and Mary shook her head.

''I've never heard you speak to a client like that before—'

'He isn't a client,' Lauranne said shortly and Mary glanced at Tom, her confusion evident.

'But he's probably the richest man in the world. And this is just the sort of challenge that you both love,' she pointed out. 'Everyone thinks Volakis is ruthless and cold and this is your chance to prove that underneath that controlled exterior lurks a warm, beating heart.'

If it hadn't been so painful, Lauranne would have laughed.

A warm, beating heart?

This was the man who had destroyed her life. He'd taken her innocent dreams and crushed them with the same ruthless lack of emotion that he applied to his business dealings.

He hadn't *believed* in her—

For a moment the pain and hurt threatened to choke her and she struggled to control her emotions, reminding herself how far she'd come since that dreadful summer five years before.

She wasn't going to let one kiss destroy that, however passionate.

'Zander Volakis doesn't have a heart. He is exactly the way he appears in the press,' she said shakily. 'He is cold-hearted and ruthless and there is nothing I or anyone else can possibly do for his public image.'

She was breathing so rapidly that she thought her lungs might explode.

Mary was still staring open-mouthed. 'I can't believe you know him—'

Lauranne felt her eyes fill and she shook her head in denial. 'I never knew him.'

She'd thought she did, but she'd been proved wrong in the most agonising, humiliating way possible.

Even now her naïvety made her blush. How could she have truly believed that a man as sophisticated and experienced as Zander Volakis would want any more from her than a brief fling? How could she have convinced herself that there was more to the relationship than sizzling sex? The man was Greek to the very backbone. His concept of relationships was different from hers. He still believed in virgin brides, mistresses and vengeance for acts of wrong.

Vengeance—

Lauranne closed her eyes, her face losing still more of its colour as she remembered the merciless way he'd dealt with her. He'd been cold and unapproachable, refusing even to listen to her. It was as if they'd never been intimate. As far as he was concerned she'd betrayed him and that was the end of it. There was no explanation that he was willing to listen to.

And seeing him so remote had hurt so badly she'd thought she'd die of the pain.

Lauranne opened her eyes. She hadn't died. She was still here and she wasn't going to let Zander Volakis destroy her a second time.

Tom glared at her. 'Tell me you won't be here at seven-thirty.'

'I won't.' Her heart rate accelerated as she remembered his promise to find her. If he wanted a chase then he was going to get one.

Tom relaxed slightly. 'And don't go home, either. You'd be too easy to find. Take my advice. Lose yourself in London. Go for a walk. Find a bar in a part of London that a style-conscious Greek billionaire wouldn't be seen dead in. Buy a wig. Dye your hair. Put on forty kilos. Spend a few nights in a seedy hotel.'

Lauranne gave a wan smile. 'And we both know that running will just make him more determined to find me. That's the way his mind works. Zander Volakis doesn't ever lose.'

But she was going to make it hard for him.

She closed her eyes briefly and sucked in a breath. What exactly did he want from her? Why would he want her to work for him? She'd already done that, five years before…

* * *

Landing a job in the public relations department of Volakis Industries immediately after she'd left university had been the most exciting thing that had ever happened to her. Lauranne had started in the London office, learning the ropes, developing a feel for the breadth of the Volakis business empire along with three other graduates, one of whom had been Tom Farrer.

As for Zander Volakis himself, she hadn't seen him. Like all the other women who worked for him, she'd drooled over his picture in the front of the annual report but hadn't had any expectations of actually meeting him in person. With offices in all the major capitals of the world, he'd flown in for meetings and left again, maintaining a punishing schedule that had left little time for mingling with anyone but his most senior staff.

She might never have met him at all if she hadn't become involved in the opening of one of his new hotels in the Caribbean.

'You're being posted there for two months,' her boss told her one morning. 'You're going to work in different departments, get a feel for the place and then you'll be in a position to entertain journalists when we arrange press visits. We call it a soft launch. The idea is to wine and dine them and generally give them such a great time that they go home and write wonderful things about the hotel and the boss. This is his flagship resort. More stars than the night sky.'

'Will he be there?' Lauranne was intrigued at the prospect of finally meeting the legendary God-like figure who had taken the wreckage of his father's company and built it into one of the most successful businesses in the world at a staggeringly young age.

'No idea.' Her boss shrugged. 'Probably not. The guy is

usually in the air. Flying from one meeting to another. Or else he's in bed with some stunning model or actress, so don't get any ideas in that direction.'

She certainly didn't have any ideas in that direction, Lauranne mused as she packed a case for the Caribbean. Just twenty-one, she had absolutely no intention of falling in love with anyone, and certainly not with Zander Volakis, no matter how good-looking and wealthy he was. The man had a wicked reputation with women and she had more sense than to fall for that sort of man.

She was sitting in the bar one evening, chatting to some of the other guests, when she was suddenly aware that she was being watched.

The man stood slightly apart from the noisy crowd, distinguished by an air of authority and by the sheer impact of his powerful physique and stunningly handsome face. She should have recognised him immediately but she didn't, perhaps because photographs in the annual report hadn't come close to capturing the vital masculinity of the man standing in front of her.

His eyes locked on hers with shocking intensity, raking over her long blonde hair with blatant male appreciation until she was breathless and trembling.

He was just *so* gorgeous.

And he couldn't take his eyes off her.

Used to keeping men at a distance, Lauranne didn't recognise the delicious excitement that suddenly burned inside her and deliberately looked away, determined to ignore him.

He was totally wrong for her.

If he was staying in the resort then he had to be seriously rich and she didn't play with billionaires, however stunning they were to look at.

All the same, she struggled to play it cool when he strolled up to her, disturbingly direct in his approach.

'I want you to have dinner with me.' He spoke perfect

English with a slight accent that just served to make his deep voice even sexier.

Struggling with temptation for the first time in her life, Lauranne was frostily polite. 'And do you always get what you want?'

The intensity of his gaze took her breath away. 'Always.'

'I'm not allowed to dine with guests—'

He dealt her a sizzling smile that made hotel rules fade to the nethermost part of her dazzled brain. 'I'm not a guest.'

She should have realised then, of course, but she didn't.

It wasn't until much, much later, when they'd talked about anything and everything and she was already half in love with him, that she noticed the deferential manner of the staff.

'Oh, my God—' She dropped her fork and her eyes widened as she finally realised exactly whom she was dining with. 'You're—you're—'

One dark eyebrow swooped upwards and his eyes glittered with amusement. 'I'm—?'

'It's you.' She swallowed, unable to look away from that disturbing gaze. 'I should have recognised you, but you don't look like the annual report.'

'A laminated brochure with forty pages?' He laughed then and she laughed too, but nervously because she was dining with a billionaire who only dated very, *very* beautiful women.

'I can't date the boss,' she croaked, transfixed by the lush thickness of his dark lashes and the slight fullness of his lower lip. 'It's against the rules.'

'But I make the rules,' he drawled lazily, dipping a strawberry in melted chocolate and leaning forward to place it between her parted lips, 'so I can either change the rules or fire you.'

And later, *much later,* he did exactly that...

*　　*　　*

Five miles away, in his flashy London office, Zander Volakis paced the floor, still brooding over his meeting with Lauranne O'Neill.

Alec watched him nervously. 'I'll find another PR company.'

Zander scowled, struggling with feelings that were totally unfamiliar. 'Why?'

Alec looked flustered. 'Because you—well, it was clear that you—the pair of you—hated each other,' he finished lamely and Zander frowned.

Totally unaccustomed to examining his emotions in any great depth, he was uncomfortably baffled as to exactly what he *was* feeling at the moment.

Hate?

He'd felt many emotions for Lauranne O'Neill, all of them shockingly basic and intense. Hatred definitely wasn't one of them.

Alec watched him, stiff and awkward. 'How long were you—er—married?'

'Four weeks, three days and six hours.' Zander gave a cynical laugh and yanked the nearest chair away from the table. 'Until then my father held the family record for the shortest marriage. Now the trophy is mine.'

'But technically you're still married,' Alec commented. 'Why did you never get a divorce?'

'Because a divorce is only necessary if you intend to marry another woman,' Zander replied grimly, sitting down and stretching long legs out in front of him, 'and I am not in the habit of repeating my mistakes.'

And because he'd pushed the whole disastrous episode firmly to the back of his mind.

Alec stared at his boss's hard expression and cleared his throat. 'Right. So presumably that's what Kouropoulos was referring to when he said that you showed no commitment to family life.'

'Four weeks, three days and six hours certainly doesn't

constitute an impressive track record,' Zander agreed
smoothly and Alec frowned.

'Well, it's a pity that we can't work with Phoenix PR.
Ex-wife or not, Lauranne O'Neill is supposed to be the best.
If anyone can persuade Kouropoulos that you're a caring
guy, she can. At the moment we can't even get him to agree
to a meeting.'

Zander stared at Alec broodingly, lean, strong fingers tapping a steady rhythm on the polished wood of the table as
he digested that piece of information.

'He *still* won't agree to a meeting?'

Alec shook his head, frustration evident as he flicked
through a pile of papers. 'It doesn't help that last week you
were photographed with a model *and* a ballet dancer. The
problem is that you don't date the same woman two nights
in a row.'

Considering the question superfluous, Zander gave a sardonic smile. 'Why would I want to?'

Alec ran a hand through his hair in a gesture of exasperation. 'Because we need to convince Kouropoulos that your
womanising is merely the mark of a desperate man searching frantically for the right woman with whom to spend the
rest of his life…except that you're married so none of that
works…' His voice trailed off as he caught the look in his
boss's eyes.

'I've never met a romantic lawyer before,' Zander observed softly. 'I pay you to deal with facts, not fiction.'

Alec gave a sigh and slumped in his chair. 'Well, in this
case the facts aren't helping. I think this is one deal we're
going to have to give up on,' he said wearily, pushing the
papers away from him and dropping his pen on top. 'Trying
to make you look like a good boy is the hardest job I've
ever been given. Just when I think I'm making progress with
our friend Kouropoulos, someone somewhere publishes
something scandalous about you and if the old guy knows
you're still married then it's no wonder he's not impressed.

This is a guy who's been with the same woman since he was twenty.'

'Presumably that's why he chooses to live on an island,' Zander said silkily. 'It restricts the opportunities for straying.

He didn't believe that any woman was capable of being faithful. If his father's experiences hadn't offered him sufficient proof, then his own certainly had.

Zander rose to his feet in a fluid movement and started pacing again.

He stopped pacing, every trace of amusement gone from his lean, handsome face. 'Be clear on one thing, Alec. I'm not giving up on this deal.'

He wouldn't rest until Blue Cove Island was his.

Alec sighed. 'There's no obvious solution.'

'Then find a less obvious one,' Zander suggested pleasantly, striding over to the window and staring down at the streets below. 'If I need a new image, then I'll get one.' He kept his back to his lawyer. 'And my wife is the woman to do it.'

There was a shocked silence.

'You're joking.'

'I never joke about business.'

'But she could do you colossal damage. The woman *hates* you—'

Remembering those incredible legs wrapped round his waist, Zander experienced an instant physical response and tightened his jaw. 'She doesn't hate me.'

She was afraid of him. Afraid of the powerful connection between them.

Alec rose to his feet, sweat clinging to his brow. 'As your lawyer I have to advise you against...' His voice tailed off under the force of that burning gaze and he shook his head. 'It's a huge risk, Zander.'

'I thrive on risk.'

'Well, I have to confess that in this case I don't understand you,' Alec confessed ruefully, shaking his head and flicking the file shut.

Zander didn't respond. He was having trouble explaining his actions to himself. For a man who prided himself on never looking backwards, he'd become uncomfortably fixated on his disastrous relationship with Lauranne. It was just because she'd refused to work for him, he reasoned, laughing silently at his own inability to ignore the challenge she'd set. Their whole relationship had been conducted in the same vein. When one of them fought, the other fought harder. It had made for a totally explosive relationship but one that had excited him more than any other.

And the prospect of even more contact filled him with a thrill of anticipation that was totally beyond his comprehension.

CHAPTER FOUR

LAURANNE glanced at her watch and realised that if she was going to take Tom's advice and lose herself in London, then it was time to move.

She slipped into the bathroom that joined onto her office and stared at her reflection in the mirror, seeing not the immaculately groomed businesswoman, but the face of the girl she'd been five years before.

Lauranne closed her eyes briefly, reflecting that, no matter how hard you worked on your external image, nothing could change the way you were inside.

Outwardly there was no sign of the innocent girl who'd fallen so crazily in love with Zander Volakis, but on the inside—on the inside that hot, wildly passionate girl that he'd discovered was still very much alive.

She lifted a hand to her mouth, touching her lower lip, *remembering*—

It had been wild. Crazy. Two months with Zander—*dark, sexual Zander*—had unlocked a part of herself that she'd carefully denied ever since and just the memories were enough to ignite a spark that warmed her body. She felt the familiar ache deep within her pelvis, a warmth, a tingling, a shockingly exciting sexual awareness that was triggered by just the mention of his name. She hadn't known it was possible for a woman to feel what Zander had made her feel.

Her feelings had been totally beyond her control, so pagan, *so basic,* that she hadn't recognised herself. Everything had seemed intensified, especially the pain of parting.

Lauranne closed her eyes and gripped the basin tightly.

If she concentrated hard enough on the parting, then the

physical need would go. She wasn't twenty-one any more and she certainly wasn't naïve.

Being with Zander hadn't just taught her about sex.

Everything she knew about pain and grief and loss she'd learned from him, and thanks to Zander she'd become an expert.

Which was why she was going to run hard in the opposite direction.

She absolutely definitely didn't want Zander Volakis to be any part of her life ever again and as soon as she could she'd see a lawyer to discuss a divorce.

Galvanised into action, she grabbed a pair of jeans from one of the cupboards, found a clean white tee shirt and changed quickly, cramming her blonde hair under a cap.

Satisfied that she looked nothing like the elegant businesswoman he'd seen earlier, she slipped her feet into a pair of flat, practical shoes and grabbed her bag.

Even if he did spot her, there was no way he'd look twice at her dressed like this. Zander mixed with truly elegant women and at the moment she looked more like a street urchin.

Outside the streets were crowded with commuters making their way home and Lauranne walked briskly away from the office and flagged a taxi, directing the driver towards the river. A walk would clear her head and she could stop for a coffee and something to eat at one of the many cafés and restaurants that overlooked the river.

The taxi dropped her off near the Houses of Parliament and she stood for a moment, watching the evening sunlight dancing on the River Thames. It was the height of summer and people hurried past, eager to get home, no one showing the slightest interest in her as she slipped on a pair of sunglasses and settled her bag on her shoulder. She felt anonymous, just another commuter on the busy streets of London, and she started to relax.

This was her home now. *Her life.* Thanks to Tom, she

had a life again. A life that was a million miles from Volakis Industries and Zander.

There was no way he was going to mess it up a second time.

'You were right, boss. She did a runner. Took a taxi to the river and then walked. She's been walking ever since. We've had a struggle not to lose her, frankly. She doesn't look anything like her photograph.'

Zander stared at his bodyguard grimly and then gave a reluctant laugh. That was so typical of Lauranne. She knew that he had the means to track her down easily but she was still stubbornly determined to make a stand. It was no wonder they always clashed so fiercely, he mused as he climbed into the back of his car and issued instructions to his driver. She was the only person he'd ever met who was as stubborn and determined as he was.

All his life, women had drooled and fawned over him, but not Lauranne. She'd ignored and disdained, forcing him to chase a woman for the first time in his life. And where other women flirted and giggled, Lauranne had argued and challenged, always emphasising their differences, driving him mad with frustration.

She was the antithesis of the woman he'd been brought up to value, so far removed from the obedient Greek woman that it was laughable. And that had been part of the attraction for him, he mused as he stared moodily out of the window. Lauranne was sparky, opinionated and difficult to handle. In fact the perfect woman for a guy who appreciated a challenge.

A slight smile on his handsome face, Zander lounged back in his seat and contemplated the prospect of doing battle with her again.

Their relationship had always been amazingly passionate and hot and seeing her today had made him realise just how much he still ached for her. His body had throbbed in the most primitive way possible and it had taken all of his legendary will-power not to spread her flat on that huge glass table that dominated her meeting room and take her hard and fast with the minimum of preliminaries.

And that was where he'd gone wrong before. He'd allowed great sex to affect his judgement. He should have just kept her in his bed until they were both too exhausted to argue.

Instead of which he'd suddenly developed a desperate urge to marry her.

And he *still* couldn't work out why he'd done that.

Aware that the car had stopped, he glanced out of the window and focused on a café with several tables placed outside overlooking the river. Scanning the tables briefly, he frowned, unable to identify her immediately, and then he looked again and a smile touched his firm mouth.

Did she really think that a baseball cap and jeans could disguise who she was? From the back she looked like a boy, but he recognised that slender neck, the slant of her narrow shoulders and the stubborn tilt of her pointed chin—

She was poised for confrontation.

Just waiting to be found so that she could spit fire and flame.

With a brief nod to his driver he stepped out of the car and strolled up to her, relishing the prospect of their encounter.

She felt him before she saw him. Sensed a change in the people around her. The atmosphere in the bustling café was suddenly highly charged. Conversations tailed off. Men sat up slightly straighter, women ceased to pay attention to their companions, their eyes fixed instead on someone behind her.

And she knew who that someone would be, of course.

Only Zander had that sort of effect on people.

Only Zander could bring an entire café to a standstill.

Wondering how far she'd get if she just stood up and ran,

she tensed, preparing herself for confrontation, refusing to look round or acknowledge his arrival in any way.

He'd found her faster than even she had anticipated. But that was Zander all over. There was no one he couldn't track down, no deal he couldn't negotiate. And with all the staff and money at his disposal, finding her must have been child's play. There was nowhere on earth she could have hidden safely if he truly wanted to find her.

But finding her didn't mean that he was going to get what he wanted.

He settled himself in the chair opposite her, utterly oblivious to the lustful looks he was attracting from the women around him.

Lauranne suppressed a bitter laugh as she recognised emotions that she herself had once felt. It wasn't just his staggering good looks that created such a stir amongst members of her sex. It was his blatant masculinity. Zander exuded an air of power and success that drew women to him like a magnet.

And she'd hated herself for falling for his charms.

Lauranne glanced around her helplessly, wanting to warn them. *You can have him,* she wanted to shout. *Have him, but beware.* He may look amazing but he's lethal and dangerous and he has absolutely no conscience.

But she didn't speak her thoughts aloud.

Instead she lifted her gaze to his, her blue eyes taunting, straight into confrontation mode. It was the only way to deal with the man. Any sign of softness and he'd walk all over her.

'Slumming it, Zander?'

He glanced around him at the simple café and gave a dismissive shrug. 'So you get to choose the battleground.'

Battleground? Reflecting that their whole relationship had been a battleground, Lauranne watched as his gaze flickered to a waiter who hurried over with almost undignified haste, one eye on the two bodyguards who hovered at a discreet distance.

She gritted her teeth and drummed her long nails on the table.

What was it about him that made men fall over themselves to do his bidding?

He'd changed out of the business suit and was dressed casually in well-cut trousers and a linen shirt and yet he was still a man in control, every inch the Greek tycoon.

The leader of the pack.

He ordered himself a coffee, satisfied himself that her drink was still full and then dismissed the waiter with a brief nod of that arrogant dark head.

She gave him an icy glare. 'So you did have me followed.'

It was a statement of fact and his dark eyes flickered with amusement as they rested on her accusing face.

'Did you think I wouldn't?'

'You wasted manpower. I have nothing to say to you, Zander, unless you want to discuss our divorce.'

'Ah, yes—divorce.' He leaned back in his chair and rested one leg over the other in a supremely masculine gesture. His aggressive jaw line was dark with the beginnings of stubble and his hair gleamed glossy black in the late evening sun. His skin was tanned to a light gold, the dark hairs visible at the neck of his shirt a tantalising reminder of just what lay underneath.

And she knew exactly what lay underneath. Against her will she found herself remembering every inch of his spectacular body in glorious, Technicolor detail and her mouth ran dry. Suddenly her fingertips seemed like the most sensitive part of her body. She wanted to touch, stroke, *scratch—*

Horrified by the explicit nature of her thoughts, she glanced away, picking up her drink and taking a large sip.

'Why haven't you instructed your solicitors before now,

I wonder?' His tone was conversational and she flattened herself against the chair, trying to create more distance between them.

'Because I don't even think about you any more,' she lied, setting her drink down so that he couldn't see how much her hand was shaking. 'Our marriage was so brief that I've all but forgotten it.'

'Is that so?' His lashes lowered and she felt her heart beat faster, wishing that she could read his thoughts. Zander had a brain that moved faster than a fighter jet.

'Yes.'

'And what about the sex, Lauranne? Have you forgotten that too?'

She curled her fingers into her palms. 'Yes.'

'So why are you shaking?' One eyebrow lifted in mockery. 'It's almost indecent, is it not,' he observed silkily, 'that despite all that has happened between us we can still want each other so desperately?'

Mortified that he'd read her so easily, she reached for her drink again but her hand was shaking so much that the contents sloshed over her fingers. 'The only thing that I want desperately is for you to go back to where you came from.'

He lounged in his chair, totally at ease with himself, thick dark lashes shielding the expression in his eyes. 'Rest assured that wherever I'm going, I'll be taking you with me.'

His words stirred something deep inside her and she stiffened her slim shoulders, determined to fight it with every breath in her body.

'Unless you're experienced at kidnapping in broad daylight, then you'll be travelling alone,' she retorted, her eyes sparking angrily as she fixed her gaze on his maddeningly handsome face. 'And I'd better warn you that I can scream *very* loudly.'

Dark eyes locked on hers, cranking up the tension another notch. 'I'm well aware of how loudly you scream, Anni,' he said softly, his voice holding a seductive quality that made her breath catch. 'And I know exactly what makes you scream.'

Anni.

She closed her eyes briefly. *He wasn't playing fair.*

Only Zander had ever called her that and even then only when they were joined in the most intimate way possible.

His use of that name now was a blatantly sexual reminder of their past.

'You're disgusting.' Her flesh burning inside and out, Lauranne put her drink down and glanced around her self-consciously.

'Would you prefer us to take this conversation somewhere more private?'

'I would prefer if you just left me alone. I'm not going anywhere with you, Zander.'

'You will, Lauranne.' His voice was a lazy drawl that played havoc with her nerve endings. 'It's good to talk to you again. I'd forgotten what it was like to be with someone who doesn't automatically agree with everything I say.'

'You *hate* it when people don't agree with you!'

'Not true.'

'Well, if you weren't such a bully people wouldn't be afraid to tell you the truth.'

He looked amused. 'You think I terrorise my staff?'

'You flatten everyone around you with the sheer force of your will, Zander,' she said bitterly. 'You're totally driven and you always, *always* have to get your own way in everything. You must have been a nightmare as a toddler.'

The change in him was so subtle that if she hadn't been so closely attuned to his every movement she would have missed it—missed the slight tightening of his sensuous mouth, the almost imperceptible narrowing of his stunning dark eyes.

Then he sat forward, back in control, reaching for the coffee that the waiter had discreetly placed on the table. 'I'm glad you realise that. It will save a great deal of unnecessary argument between us.'

'Every argument we've ever had has been totally necessary.'

'That's not how I remember it.'

She lifted her chin. 'Then you have a very selective memory.'

'My memory is faultless. Especially where you're concerned. I remember every row we had, every accusation you flung at me and every word you gasped when we made love.'

The air thumped out of her lungs. 'Then you must have a truly amazing memory,' she said hoarsely, 'because our relationship was one big endless row.'

'Because you refused to do anything without a fight. Even sex was a fight.'

His eyes gleamed and Lauranne felt heat break out on her skin, remembering just exactly how the sex had been. Totally wild. Frantic. Beyond any sort of control. There had been nothing tranquil or gentle about their relationship. It had been hot and antagonistic and confrontational from the first day they'd met.

'And you always expected everything to go your way,' she croaked, ignoring the burning heat that flared low in her pelvis. 'Just because women usually fall at your feet, you thought that just one glance in my direction would be enough to have me joining them. You thought that one click of your fingers would have me running to do your bidding.'

'So you made it your life's mission to do the opposite,' he said dryly, raising his cup in a mock salute. 'You burned for me as badly as I burned for you, but you tortured us both with your elaborate games.'

'They weren't games. We're different people, Zander, from different cultures. You believe in virgin brides and m-mistresses—' she stumbled over the word and then lifted

her chin defiantly '—and I believe that a relationship between a man and a woman should be equal.'

His face hardened. 'So what were you doing with Farrer?
He's not even close to being your equal—'

She stood up so suddenly that her chair would have fallen
had he not snaked out a lean brown hand and caught it, the
speed of his reaction breathtaking.

'You were the one who insisted that we didn't mention
Tom's name,' she hissed, her heart pounding with reaction.
'You're breaking your own rules, Zander.'

'Sit down.' He didn't raise his voice but she froze, held
immobile by the sheer force of his presence.

'No.' Tears pricked behind her eyes and she blinked them
away, furious with herself, determined not to display any
weakness in front of this man. 'I'm not enjoying the conversation.'

'You have a choice.' His tone was pleasant but there was
no missing the steely undertone. 'Either we can talk here,
or we can talk in the privacy of my hotel.'

Which, roughly translated, meant that the only thing that
was negotiable was the venue. And after what had happened
that afternoon there was absolutely no way she'd choose to
be alone with him.

Her blue eyes sparked angrily. 'So in other words I have
no choice at all.'

He dismissed her accusation with a careless lift of those
broad shoulders. 'If that's the way you choose to see it.'

The waiter brought more drinks at that moment and she
sat down again, fuming, watching while he fussed around
Zander, checking that he had everything he wanted.

When they were finally left alone Zander took a mouthful
of coffee and pulled a face.

'The coffee is disgusting,' he said mildly. 'I shall be glad
to be back in Greece.'

'So go,' she suggested sweetly and he smiled.

'I intend to. But before I go, I have work to do. And so have you.'

She returned his gaze coldly. 'I already told you, I'm not interested.'

'Really?' He leaned back in his chair, totally relaxed and in control, his eyes not leaving her face as he suddenly produced some papers. 'A list of your clients, Lauranne. Amazing how many of them bank with me.'

Lauranne felt her face drain of colour. She'd forgotten just how diverse his business interests were. Or perhaps she'd never really known. 'You wouldn't—'

He smiled. 'Oh, but I would, *agape mou.*'

Her heart was thumping hard against her chest and the dampness of her palms had nothing to do with the warmth of the summer evening.

Saying no to Zander was like trying to stop an approaching tidal wave by raising a hand.

'Why would you possibly want me to work for you?'

'Because I need to change my public image. And I need to do it fast.'

She gave a humourless laugh. 'You mean people are finally finding out what you're really like. The ruthless businessman routine wearing a little thin, is it, Zander?'

His gaze didn't flicker but she saw a dangerous glint in his dark eyes and felt a shiver of apprehension.

Whatever she thought of him, Zander was a formidable opponent and she'd be a fool to underestimate him.

'I can't help you.' She stiffened her shoulders and forced herself to look him in the eye. 'My job is to discover and reveal the softer side of people, to make them seem more human, more approachable. But we both know that you don't have a soft side, Zander. You've earned your reputation for being ruthless and unemotional and there's nothing I can do to change that.'

He looked at her, his gaze impassive. 'So you don't mind if Tom loses the business?'

She swallowed hard, studying the man who had dominated her whole life since the day she'd met him. 'You'd really do it, wouldn't you?'

'I want you to work for me, Lauranne.' He gave a dismissive shrug. 'If that's what it takes—'

She gave a disbelieving laugh. 'And you want me to persuade people that you're soft and caring?'

'I'm a businessman. Soft and caring aren't qualities that would benefit my business,' he said dryly, 'but I want you to show a more human side, yes. And I'm willing to forget the past, if that's what's bothering you.'

She looked at him incredulously, fighting an impulse to slap his face. He obviously thought he was being generous.

'You're unbelievable, Zander.' She gave a humourless laugh, her fingers tightening on the arms of her chair. 'You threw me out and you wrecked my career and you expect us just to carry on as if nothing had happened?'

He gave a casual shrug of his broad shoulders. 'I've moved on.'

Moved on.

She looked at him helplessly, stricken by his careless dismissal of what they'd shared. If she'd needed any evidence that their relationship had meant nothing to him then she had it now. *If only it were that easy for her.* 'Why are you doing this?' Despite all her efforts, her voice shook. 'Why me, Zander?'

'Because I've seen what you've achieved for other clients,' he responded smoothly and she frowned suspiciously.

'Why do you need to change your image, anyway? You've never cared what people think of you.'

His handsome face gave nothing away. 'I'm working on a deal. It's important to me.' His long fingers fiddled with his coffee cup. 'The owner is ridiculously sentimental about the business he's selling. He doesn't believe I'm capable of understanding family values.'

'Evidently a wise man,' Lauranne said, her blue eyes

sparking as she looked at him. 'He obviously isn't impressed by your lack of morals. All you're interested in is a quick lay.'

His eyes didn't leave hers. 'When I make love to a woman it's never, ever quick.' His voice was a slow, sexy drawl that made her breathing stop, her brain jammed with memories so provocative that the world around her disappeared and her entire focus was him. 'You of all people should remember that, Lauranne.'

She did remember that.

And so did her body. Awareness throbbed through her veins and she could tell from the streak of colour touching his incredible bone structure that he was remembering it too.

She gazed into those compelling dark eyes and felt her temperature rise. He was shockingly, hotly handsome and no matter how many warnings her brain sent out, her body refused to listen.

Desperate to get away from him while she still could, she rose to her feet again, her chair scraping on the ground.

'Well, it's been fascinating talking to you, Zander, but I really have to go now.'

'We haven't finished.' His calm tone was totally at odds with the dangerous glint in his eyes.

'We're in a public place,' she pointed out, wishing that she felt as confident as she sounded. 'And I *have* finished.'

He sat back in his chair, his eyes glittering. 'Sit down, Lauranne.'

Her eyes clashing mutinously with his, she tried to step away from the table but a lean brown hand snaked out and caught her wrist, jerking her off balance so that she landed in his lap.

Her gasp of protest was smothered by the hot demands of his mouth, the erotic slide of his tongue sending delicious waves of excitement coursing through her.

His kiss was hot and compelling and it was only when

he slowly detached his mouth from hers that she realised that her fingers had slid into his silky dark hair.

Mortified by this visible evidence of her instinctive response to him, she released him instantly. Staring at him in mute horror, she tried to scoot off his lap but he held her easily; a wry smile played around his firm mouth.

'I think you'd better stay where you are for now,' he said huskily, and she shivered as she recognised the timbre of his voice. She'd teased him about it on so many occasions. About the fact that he sounded *so* Greek when he was aroused.

She felt the hard heat of him through the fabric of his trousers and closed her eyes.

He was aroused now. Very aroused.

And so was she.

'Zander—' Her voice sounded strangled as she tried to ignore the delicious lethargy that spread through her body. 'What are you doing?'

'Jogging your memory,' he said silkily, his arms tightening around her. 'You said that you had all but forgotten our relationship. I'm told that a shock can cure amnesia.'

'It can also kill people,' she gritted, trying to ignore his hard strength and the traitorous throb deep in her pelvis. 'What is it you want from me?'

'I want you to help me close this deal.' His voice was soft, so that to the casual observer it would have seemed as though he were murmuring words of love. 'I want you to do whatever it takes to convince Kouropoulos that I'm a warm, sensitive guy who is capable of understanding what makes a family resort run smoothly.'

Her eyes flew wide and she stared at him in disbelief. 'I'm a PR consultant, not a magician. And we both know you're neither warm nor sensitive.'

He smiled, maddeningly unperturbed by her horrified reaction. 'Parts of me are extremely sensitive.'

She felt the blush touch her cheeks and looked at him sickly. 'I won't do it.'

'Yes, you will.' He leaned forward and brushed a strand of blonde hair away from her face with deceptively gentle fingers. 'You will. You'll do it because it's the only way you'll get your divorce. And because if you don't, my English beauty,' he said softly, 'I'll ruin you for a second time. And this time I'll ruin Farrer too.'

CHAPTER FIVE

'THE girl's a genius.' Alec threw another newspaper down on the table and looked at Zander with astonishment. 'In less than two weeks she's managed to have you featured on all the major TV channels and you've been in almost every newspaper that matters. And there hasn't been one picture of you dating glamorous women. How have you managed it?'

'I have had an exceedingly boring fortnight,' Zander drawled, his handsome face blank of expression as he scanned the pile of newspapers that his secretary had left on his desk. He had no intention of revealing the truth to his lawyer. That the past two weeks had been anything but boring. Stimulating and sexually charged were words that came to mind. Certainly not boring.

He'd started out intending to punish Lauranne by making her work for him but he'd ended up punishing himself equally.

His entire body was throbbing with frustration.

Alec laughed. 'Well, it worked. Suddenly you're Mr Nice Guy.' He squinted down at one particular article with interest. 'I never knew you donated so much money to those children's charities.'

Zander tensed. 'Because I don't donate money as a publicity stunt,' he said shortly. 'Revealing it wasn't my choice but apparently she spoke to someone in Corporate Affairs and they gave her a list of my charitable donations.'

Alec shrugged. 'Either way, she's certainly achieved way in excess of our expectations. I'm amazed she agreed to help given the fact that you fired her. How did you talk her into it?'

'I was—persuasive.' Zander glanced at the last of the newspapers, his expression neutral and Alec gave a wry smile.

'In other words you didn't take no for an answer. So is that it?'

'Apart from the première this evening.'

Alec looked at him in surprise. 'You're going to that?'

Zander gave a ghost of a smile. 'Of course. And this time I intend to be photographed with a woman. The right woman.'

And he was looking forward to it enormously.

'You're taking Lauranne?' Alec looked shocked. 'Why? There haven't been any photos of you in the papers for two weeks. Why do it now? And with her?'

'I have my reasons.' And he had absolutely no intention of divulging them to anyone, least of all his lawyer. 'And now I want you to ring Kouropoulos and set up a meeting.'

Alec fiddled with the papers. 'He might not agree of course, he could still—'

'He'll agree.'

Alec lifted his chin, his expression suddenly keen. 'But we haven't—'

'He'll agree.'

Alec opened his mouth and then closed it again, suddenly brisk and professional. 'Right. I'll speak to his lawyers now.'

'Good.' Zander stood up and snapped the file shut. 'I'm flying to Blue Cove Island tonight after the première.'

Alec gave the wan smile of someone well aware that he was facing a challenge. 'I'll tell him that.' He glanced at his boss, unusually hesitant. 'You look stressed. You've been working punishing hours. Maybe—'

'I always work punishing hours.' Zander interrupted him impatiently and Alec gave a slight frown.

'But I've never seen you stressed before.'

Zander lifted an eyebrow, his expression dangerous. 'Are you my lawyer or my doctor?'

Alec coloured slightly. 'I just thought maybe all the press attention—' he risked a slight smile '—the strain of being a good boy for two whole weeks…'

Zander gave a reluctant smile, thinking that his lawyer was closer to the truth than he imagined.

Two weeks of being in close contact with Lauranne had left him pulsing with a sexual frustration so powerful that he was in a state of almost permanent discomfort. Whether they'd been in television studios, or meeting journalists for interviews, she'd been hovering in the background, immaculately dressed, her blonde hair fastened firmly on top of her head. He'd found it harder and harder to concentrate on the interviews, his eyes and brain totally preoccupied by the woman on the other side of the lights. Only the constant presence of other people in the room had prevented him from hauling her into his arms and stripping the elegant business suit from her perfect body.

Not accustomed to denying himself sexually, Zander was finding the enforced period of celibacy increasingly frustrating.

Realising that Alec was still looking at him oddly, he swore softly in Greek. 'I'm fine. Just set up that meeting.'

Supremely confident that there wasn't a business deal that he couldn't successfully negotiate if given the opportunity, he strode out of the room leaving his lawyer to sort out the details.

'So you turned him into Mr Perfect.' Tom poured himself a coffee and slumped into a chair opposite her huge glass desk. 'I can't believe you agreed to do that work for him. And not only that but you've managed to achieve a miracle. You managed to make the bastard look good.'

Lauranne stared blankly at the stack of newspapers on her

desk, all featuring Zander Volakis in an unusually flattering light.

In normal circumstances she would have felt immensely proud of the job she'd done portraying him as a warm, caring man but these weren't normal circumstances. She'd done it to protect Tom.

And to get a divorce.

'I just wanted to get the job over with,' she muttered and Tom lifted an eyebrow.

'So is that it, or is he coming back for more?'

'Just the première tonight.'

'He's taking *you?*' Tom narrowed his eyes, instantly on the alert. 'Excuse me, but you've spent the last two weeks removing every speck of dust from his reputation and now he wants to turn up at a public event with his *estranged wife?* Doesn't this strike you as odd?'

'Not really. It's just business. And after tonight, there's no more.' Lauranne licked her lips and tucked a strand of blonde hair behind her ear. 'He wanted quick results and he's had them. As far as I'm concerned the campaign is finished. He's done interviews for just about everyone and if they haven't used the story already then they'll use it soon.'

'I couldn't believe that interview I saw on TV this morning.' Tom curled his fingers around his coffee mug and shook his head in disbelief. 'He came across as warm and caring. I found myself wanting to work for the guy, and I know what he's like. How the hell did you do it?'

'It's my job,' Lauranne said shortly, 'and I managed to dig up some good stuff.' She frowned slightly. A surprising amount of good stuff, if she was honest. 'His employees didn't have a bad word to say about him.'

'Then you were obviously speaking to the wrong ones. I was his employee once,' Tom gritted, 'and I can certainly think of a bad word. In fact I can think of several bad words. How many would you like?'

Lauranne tried to smile, but her expression was troubled. 'He gives away a small fortune, Tom, and he doesn't tell people.' She chewed her lip. 'Even his own staff don't know.'

And almost all of it to children's charities. She wondered if there was a reason behind that.

'So?' Tom shot her an incredulous look. 'Tell me you're not going all gooey on me. He's a billionaire, Lauranne. He can give away millions and not notice. It doesn't make him a good guy. Wake up.'

Lauranne pulled herself together. 'I'm awake. I know it doesn't make him a good guy.'

He was a guy who would resort to blackmail if it suited him.

But she couldn't push away the image of Zander, an unusually discomforted Zander, being questioned about his charitable donations. He hadn't wanted to discuss it and instead had skilfully switched the topic of conversation to the needs of the charities that he supported, focusing on the work they were doing rather than the finance that he poured into their coffers. And of course it helped that he was movie-star handsome. The cameras had loved him, the harsh studio lighting only emphasising his perfect bone structure and glossy dark hair as he spoke with an ease and confidence that just increased his appeal.

Remembering just how great that appeal had been, Lauranne reminded herself that it was all part of his act. Zander was the ultimate negotiator, a skilled operator who knew exactly how to manipulate people and situations to his advantage.

Tom took a sip of coffee. 'What I still don't understand,' he said slowly, 'is why you agreed to do it.'

Lauranne didn't meet his eyes. She still hadn't told him the truth. Hadn't told him about Zander's threat to put them out of business.

Tom was her best friend and she owed him.

'It just seemed easier than refusing,' she said finally, dredging up a smile with an effort. 'And after tonight it will be finished.'

She still had to get through one more evening but at least they'd be in public again. Crowds were her protection.

'Is it?' Tom stared at her broodingly. 'I have a feeling that this thing with you and Zander will never be finished. Not while the pair of you are living on the same planet and breathing the same air.'

'There is no thing between us.' Lauranne stood up abruptly and glanced at her watch. 'I'm going home. I have to get changed before tonight. He's picking me up at seven.'

'Good luck.' Tom gave a weary smile. 'Don't forget to smile for the cameras when your feet hit that red carpet. And get ready for trouble. When word gets out that you're his wife, there'll be a feeding frenzy.'

'Word isn't going to get out,' Lauranne said, picking up her bag. 'Why would anyone be interested in me?'

'Because you're with him,' Tom said dryly. 'Be on your guard. Volakis never does anything without a reason. If he's taking you tonight, then there's a reason.'

'He needs a partner,' Lauranne said, wishing that she could push away the uneasy suspicion that Tom might be right.

Was Zander playing some elaborate game?

Tom stood up, his expression grim. 'Did he kiss you again?'

Lauranne shook her head.

He hadn't needed to.

Just being in the same room as him had such an intense effect on her physically that she couldn't concentrate on anything except him. They hadn't been able to take their eyes off each other, the sexual awareness between them rising to such an intensity that she was amazed that the journalists hadn't picked up on it. Tension had throbbed around them like a force field, isolating them from everyone else.

'Of course he didn't kiss me.' Lauranne walked towards the door, wondering if a cold shower would help. 'Fortunately we were surrounded by cameramen and journalists and every living, breathing female within a million miles of London who could find an excuse to be there.' She hadn't been on her own with him for a single second and she was grateful for that. She didn't trust him. And she certainly didn't trust herself. She'd come to the conclusion that her body had lousy judgement. 'And after tonight I won't be seeing him again.'

And for that she was eternally thankful.

Maybe, just maybe, if she concentrated hard enough, she'd be able to get him out of her mind and get on with her life.

There *had* to be men out there who wouldn't pale next to Zander—

Tom glanced out of the window. 'The sky is looking pretty dark. Do you need a lift home?'

Lauranne shook her head. 'No, thanks. I need the fresh air. I'll walk part of the way and then grab a cab if it rains. See you tomorrow.'

She walked out of her office and took the lift down to the ground floor.

The moment she stepped out onto the pavement she saw the car. Sleek, dark and complete with uniformed driver. Zander lounged against the rear passenger door, waiting for her, his security staff hovering at a discreet distance.

Zander the hunter.

'Get in.' Thick dark lashes framing his disturbingly intent gaze, he straightened and extended a lean brown hand towards the car in invitation. 'I'll give you a lift home. It will give you more time to get ready for tonight.'

It was the first time she'd been alone with him since they'd started the campaign and during that time the tension between them had risen to fever pitch. Being in a car alone with him was the last thing she wanted. It was as if she'd been admiring a tiger safely in captivity only to find that it had escaped and was now confronting her.

Her mouth was dry and her heart was pounding against her chest. What was it they said about dangerous situations? Fight or flight. Well, flight was a waste of time where Zander was concerned because he always caught up with her. Which just left fight.

Angling her chin, she looked at him with ill-disguised hostility. 'I'm walking home. I need the fresh air.'

There was no way she was climbing into a car with him.

'Then I'll walk with you.' With a discreet jerk of his dark head he dismissed his bodyguards and chauffeur and strolled alongside her, ignoring the furious look she cast in his direction.

'I prefer to walk alone.'

As usual he ignored her, adjusting his pace to match hers. 'Surely it's usual for a client to have a debrief after such an intensive campaign?'

It was usual, but she didn't want to spend any more time with Zander than she had to. She needed to spend some time on her own, reminding herself of all the reasons why she should be avoiding him. Two weeks in his company had seriously affected her judgement.

'But you're not really a client,' she said. 'You're just a man who resorts to blackmail.'

He smiled, not in the least disturbed by her less-than-flattering analysis of his character. 'So I am.'

She quickened her pace, forcing herself to look straight ahead. To glance sideways was to court temptation and she didn't trust herself. Even without looking she was painfully conscious of every male inch of him as he strolled next to her. Her feminine senses in a state of high alert, she almost jumped as she felt the tantalising brush of his arm against hers.

Suddenly it was too much. Her whole body was on fire with anticipation.

'I have nothing to say to you, Zander.' She sounded breathless, as if she'd been running for her life, and if she had any sense then that was exactly what she should be doing, she reflected helplessly. She had to get away from him if she was going to preserve her sanity. Her job. *Her life.* 'I did as you asked and after tonight I want you to leave me alone. I don't want to see you again. And I'll be instructing my lawyer.'

As she finished speaking she felt the first drops of rain on her head and her shoulders and then suddenly the rain started to fall heavily, hammering the pavement and drenching unprepared commuters.

Squinting through damp lashes, Lauranne frantically scanned the traffic-clogged streets for a taxi but as usual there was no sign of one and in seconds they were soaked.

Swearing in Greek, Zander lifted a hand in an imperious gesture and moments later the sleek dark car pulled up alongside the kerb and he was driving her forwards, the warmth of his hand branding the small of her back.

For a moment Lauranne dug her heels in, resisting both that pressure and his arrogant assumption that she'd go where he led. She preferred to take her chances with the weather than climb into the intimate confines of a car with a man as lethally attractive as Zander.

He stared at her with naked exasperation, raindrops clinging to seductively thick lashes as he ran fingers through his dripping hair with the incredulity of someone accustomed to living in a hot climate. '*Theos mou,* this is *not* the time to argue. If you must argue then at least do it somewhere dry. Get in before we both drown.'

Driven by the sheer force of his personality, Lauranne slid reluctantly into the vehicle and was immediately swallowed up by the warmth and comfort of his car.

Zander delivered several instructions in rapid Greek and then stretched out a lean brown hand and hit a button somewhere to his right, activating a screen between him and his driver.

And only then was she aware that her thin silk blouse was now transparent, the delicate lace of her bra clearly visible through the soaked fabric.

Her face hot with embarrassment, Lauranne huddled in the far corner of the seat, trying to put as much distance between her and Zander as possible. Being alone with him in the confines of a car made her struggle for breath.

There was a long, burning silence and when he finally spoke his voice was deep and very, very male.

'Only English rain can drown you in seconds,' he drawled, reaching under one of the seats and pulling out a drawer that contained several towels. 'Come here.'

She put up a feeble resistance but he ignored her, removing the clip that held her hair in place at the back of her head and rubbing her soaked hair with firm, determined strokes. Exactly when his movements changed she wasn't sure but she gradually became aware that the rhythm and pressure had altered subtly from practical to seductive.

She sat still, hypnotised by the steady pounding of rain on the roof of the car and the touch of his hands. Gradually the sound of the rain faded into the background, eclipsed by the pounding of her heart and the snatch of her breath. They were totally alone, the plush interior of the car creating an atmosphere of intimacy that suffocated her resolve. Drawn in by the sizzling awareness that burned between them, Lauranne was suddenly controlled by her senses. She felt the slide of smooth leather under her bare thigh, heard the harshness of his breathing and saw the dampness of his shirt clinging to his powerful body.

So it wasn't just *her* clothes that were now see-through, she reflected dizzily, her mouth drying as she found herself eye-level with his broad chest.

Through his rain-soaked shirt she could see the shadow of dark body hair, a tantalising reminder of the masculine perfection of his body, which had once been so achingly familiar—

He dropped the towel on the floor and smoothed her tangled hair away from her face, the pad of his thumb caressing her flushed cheeks. She lifted her gaze to his and dark eyes locked onto hers with a simmering intensity that made her breath catch. And still his thumb caressed her cheek in a movement so seductive that her lips parted in mute invitation.

They stared at each other for endless seconds and then his gaze shifted, raking the soft swell of her breasts, clearly visible through the damp material.

Like someone in shock, Lauranne sat immobile, unable to persuade her body to do any of the things her brain was suggesting.

Run.

Slap him.

Kiss him.

They both knew it was coming, of course. It had been coming since the day he strode back into her life two weeks earlier and her entire body ached for the satisfaction that only he could give her. So much so that when he muttered a raw imprecation and brought his mouth down hard on hers, she sobbed with relief and leaned into him, desperate for him to kiss her as only he knew how.

She curled her fingers into the damp fabric of his shirt, shivering as she felt the hard, masculine flesh beneath. He framed her face with his hands, holding her captive as he kissed her with a forceful hunger that sent shock waves of liquid excitement coursing through her body. Her head slammed back against the seat under the pressure of his and she felt his hand slide up and touch the bare skin of her inner thigh.

'I've been longing to do this for two weeks,' he groaned, shifting her body so that she was virtually lying underneath him. 'Every time I turned round you were standing there in your perfect suit with your hair up—'

His breathing decidedly unsteady, he kissed her neck, finding that sensitive spot just behind her ear, and then worked his way back to her mouth, the erotic invasion so explicitly sexual that Lauranne sank her hands into his glossy dark hair, frantic to maintain the contact.

'I wanted you too—' She gasped the words against his seeking mouth and he kissed her as though it was to be their last kiss, their last contact as man and woman, and she matched his desperation, tongue for tongue, bite for bite, in an undisciplined mating that was totally out of control.

'Anni—' The intimate version of her name transported her back in time to the heat of a Caribbean beach in the moonlight.

Her fingers wrenched at his shirt, losing buttons in her frantic haste to be closer to him. And then finally his shirt was open and she slid her hands over his sleek, bronze flesh, shivering in a purely feminine response to his masculine strength.

She whimpered his name and he licked into her mouth, stealing the words, her breath and her will-power.

She felt the thrust of his body against hers, the thickness of his erection pressing through the fabric of his trousers and she lifted against him, instinctively drawing closer to his masculine heat.

A ferocious need engulfed her and it was only when he dragged his mouth away from hers and muttered something in Greek that she realised that they were close to making love in the back of his car.

His eyes fierce with passion, he gazed down at her, his breathing unsteady. '*Theos mou,* I don't *know* myself with you,' he groaned. 'I start off wanting to punish you and end up punishing myself.'

Punish her?

He wanted to punish her?

Utterly disorientated, she stared up at him dizzily, looking first at the dark curls that shadowed his muscular chest and then at the streaks of colour that touched his hard cheekbones. Her whole body throbbed with unfulfilled need, ached with a desire so powerful that she had to struggle not to grab him again and beg him to make love to her. For a brief moment she wondered where he'd found the willpower to stop. But he had. And his cool-headed ability to end the contact between them with so little effort suddenly quenched her own frantic response.

Gradually the harsh reality of what they'd done—what *she'd* done—intruded on her sex-induced stupor.

She pushed at his broad chest and he shifted, something unfamiliar blazing in his eyes as he looked at her. It occurred to her that he certainly didn't *look* cool.

'We shouldn't have done that.' Lauranne scooted away from him, shredded by humiliation, her cheeks flaming red as she tugged her skirt down over her exposed thighs. 'I-it was a mistake.'

'I agree. My car is *not* the place,' he said savagely, raking long fingers through sleek dark hair in a very obvious effort to regain control. 'Let's end this farce and go back to my hotel.'

His intention was quite explicit and she shook her head.

'No!' Her lips were swollen and tingling from the heat of his kiss, every secret corner of her body awakened by his touch. 'It's not the car. It's you. Me. It isn't what I want.'

He sucked in a breath, still visibly aroused and battling with his baser instincts.

'Not what you want?' As he registered her words he shot her an incredulous look. 'So what was that all about? You were ripping my clothes off in case I caught a chill?'

Breathtakingly aware of his bare chest still within touching distance, she forced herself to look away. Forced herself to resist temptation—

'Of course not—' she was too shocked by her own fevered response to be anything but honest with him '—but it isn't right, Zander, and you know it.'

He frowned. 'It was totally right. It was what we both want and if I hadn't called a halt then we would now be making love on the back seat of my car.'

His less-than-subtle reminder that it had been *him* that had stopped it made her want to sink into a dark hole. She was just so vulnerable to him and she hated herself for it. Hated herself for her lack of control.

She looked at him and then wished she hadn't as her eyes homed in greedily on his sexy mouth and the darkness of his very masculine jaw. If ever a man had been designed to tempt a woman it was Zander Volakis.

Maybe she needed to face the fact that she'd *never* be immune to him.

'All right. It was you that called a halt,' she admitted bravely, 'but there's more to a relationship than sex. We're opposites, Zander.'

'And opposites attract,' he said dryly, 'as we seem to prove every time we meet.'

'They also make each other's lives miserable,' she pointed out with a humourless laugh. 'We're too different.'

'Differences are good. It's the differences that make our relationship so exciting, *agape mou.*' He lounged back in his seat, totally relaxed, the expression in his eyes shielded by thick, dark lashes. 'You're totally unpredictable and you always surprise me. And I look forward to being surprised again and again.'

'No!' She said the word to herself as much as him, trying to remind herself of the havoc that this man had created in her life and in her heart. 'Do you really think I'd sleep with you after everything that's happened?'

'Why not?' He lifted broad shoulders in a casual shrug. 'We're both consenting adults and we share a powerful attraction. I've already told you that I'm willing to forget the past. Why shouldn't you?'

'Because our marriage is over!'

He smiled, maddeningly unperturbed by her passionate outburst. 'Stop changing the subject.'

'I *hated* you—'

'And I hated you back.'

She closed her eyes. 'So stop this car and let me out. While we're both still relatively sane.'

He gave a short laugh. 'I think sanity deserted us both that night we met on the beach.'

'We should never have married—' She muttered the words, wanting him to deny them but knowing that he wouldn't. Zander had been involved with some of the most beautiful women in the world. Why had she ever expected him to stay faithful to *her?*

'But we did.' His eyes glittered and she closed her eyes, a vision of being Zander's lover exploding inside her brain with a vividness that was as disconcerting as it was unwelcome.

'Our relationship was a disaster.'

'Our relationship was fine until you slept with Farrer.'

She flinched. 'I did not sleep with Tom!'

'You were in bed together.'

She looked at him in outrage, wondering how he had the nerve to accuse her of being unfaithful when he'd been the one sleeping with another woman.

'It's true that I kissed him,' she confessed finally, 'but we never slept together. We've only ever been friends. I kissed him because I wanted to hurt you the way you'd hurt me.'

There was a loaded silence and when he finally spoke his voice was cold. 'Why did you want to hurt me?'

Because she'd expected fidelity and what she'd been given was betrayal.

This was the time to tell him what she'd seen. To tell him why she'd rushed to Tom. *To tell him just how much he'd hurt her.*

She opened her mouth and then closed it again. What was the point? It was all five years too late.

'It doesn't matter now,' she said wearily. 'But for the record, I never had an affair with Tom. And it was me that kissed him, not the other way round. I wanted you to think it was something more.'

His eyes hardened. 'You were in each other's arms.'

'We were friends. I was upset. He was comforting me.'

'We were lovers,' Zander shot back relentlessly, his mouth set in a grim line. 'If you needed comfort then I should have been the one comforting you.'

But he'd been the cause of her distress. But she'd never once confronted him with his infidelity. And after that ghastly moment when he'd walked in on her and Tom her whole life had unravelled with alarming speed.

'There is *nothing* between Tom and I.'

For Tom's sake, she wanted to get that straight. The rest of it didn't matter any more.

'The guy is in love with you.' It was a statement of fact, delivered without a shred of emotion, and Lauranne shook her head.

'You're so wrong.'

Maybe Tom had been a little bit in love with her at one time, but there had *never* been anything between them.

Zander stared back at her, lean fingers tapping rhythmically on his muscular thigh. 'I used to notice him watching you.' His tone was conversational but something in his eyes stopped the breath in her lungs. 'If you hadn't been so fond of him I would have blacked his eye eight weeks earlier.'

Her heart was thumping so hard she was aware of every beat. 'You're an animal—'

'You were *mine*.'

For endless seconds they stared at each other and Lauranne felt a treacherous warmth spread through her veins. *What was wrong with her?* His possessive statement felt good when it should have felt bad, the sheer force of his personality melting a resolve that should have been as hard as steel.

'I was never yours.'

'No?' His voice was barely audible and she gazed at him, hypnotised by the look in his eyes. 'When we ran hand in hand across the sandy beach to find somewhere secluded just so that we could laugh and talk about everything in private, were you mine then?'

It was as if he'd pressed her face against a mirror, reflecting her own thoughts and memories in glorious Technicolor.

She swallowed. 'Zander—'

'Or when we shared a romantic dinner of lobster and wine on my terrace, both so hot for each other that we could barely eat. Were you mine then?'

She opened her mouth but no sound came out.

'Or that first night we came together as a man and a woman,' he said hoarsely, leaning towards her as he spoke, 'you wound your arms round my neck and told me that you trusted me. And when I finally thrust inside you, you sobbed my name, Anni. *My* name. Were *you mine* then?'

She'd thought she was.

Dear God, she'd wanted to be…

Lauranne bit her lip, still not trusting herself to speak.

It had been so unbelievably good—

'Which brings me back to my original question,' he said, relentless in his pursuit of an answer, 'which was why you turned to Tom instead of me.'

Finally she found her voice. 'Because *you* were the problem.' Her blue eyes flashed with reproach and accusation. How dared he be so self-righteous when *he'd* been the one in the wrong? 'Because you are just *so* Greek. You talk about fidelity but you know *nothing* about fidelity yourself and you certainly don't understand women. Why do you think I married you?'

'Unlimited access to my credit card?'

She stared at him, stunned into silence by his cynical

assessment of their doomed marriage. 'You think I married you for your *money?*'

He shrugged. 'Why else?'

Because she'd loved him. She'd loved him so much that the emotion had completely overwhelmed her.

But he'd *never* loved her. And she'd always known that, but at the time she'd thought that she loved him enough to compensate.

She'd been wrong.

Matching his careless attitude, she stuck her chin in the air. 'Just for the record I'm going to tell you one more time that I did *not* sleep with Tom!'

'And just for the record I'm going to tell you one more time that I don't believe you.'

'And I don't even care any more,' she shot back. 'It's history. And you and I are history. The gap between us is so wide that even a ferry couldn't cross it. And now let me out of this car. After tonight I never want to see you again.'

She thumped on the window that separated them from the driver and he pulled over instantly. Knowing that even the slightest hesitation would be disastrous, Lauranne was out of the door while the car was still moving. She heard Zander swear softly in Greek, registered that he tried to stop her, but hit the pavement running and vanished into the crowd.

CHAPTER SIX

ZANDER paced the floor of his hotel suite, simmering with barely contained frustration as he tried to unravel the mysteries of female conversation.

What the hell had Lauranne meant by telling him that he didn't understand women?

He understood women perfectly.

Or, rather, he understood *most* women, he admitted, grinding his teeth together as he turned and paced back again. The problem was that Lauranne was definitely not most women.

What exactly had she meant about that comment that he was 'so Greek'? Of course he was Greek!

And why had she made that wildly passionate remark about wanting to hurt him and him not understanding fidelity when it had been *her* infidelity that had ultimately pushed them apart?

Zander poured himself a large whiskey and stared out of the huge glass windows that afforded him a perfect view of London. An ominous frown darkened his sharply drawn features as he pondered the facts.

Finding her with Farrer had induced a jealousy so ferocious in its intensity that he hadn't stopped to question what he'd seen. He hadn't thought it needed questioning. Until this evening.

He downed the whiskey in one mouthful, forcing himself to confront the unpalatable possibility that he'd overreacted and misjudged the situation.

For a man who prided himself on his ability to make rational, unemotional decisions, acknowledging the degree of emotion he'd employed in ending his relationship with Lauranne left him feeling distinctly uncomfortable.

Her remark about needing comfort still hovered in his mind, refusing to go away.

Why had she needed comfort? She'd been in a hotly passionate relationship with *him*. The fact that she might have turned to another man for comfort angered him as much as the concept that she might have had an affair.

Zander ground his teeth with frustration, feeling as though he were confronted by a giant, complex jigsaw puzzle with half the pieces missing and no clue as to the final picture.

'Why do you think I married you?'

He stared thoughtfully into the empty glass, unable to ignore the fact that Lauranne had never shown any interest in money or possessions. On the few occasions he'd wanted to buy her something she'd refused to let him and he'd dismissed her reluctance to spend his money as another example of her stubborn nature. All the other women in his acquaintance had made spending an art form. Only Lauranne had shown absolutely no interest in his money.

But then Lauranne was cleverer than most women.

Had their marriage lasted longer then she doubtless would have shopped till she dropped. Didn't they all?

But in the five years they'd been apart she'd never asked him for a penny. Instead she'd turned to Farrer.

He gritted his teeth.

And she expected him to believe that she hadn't slept with the guy?

He was still dealing with the knowledge that another man had been financially responsible for *his wife* when there was a tap on the door.

A thrill of anticipation ran through his veins and he was across the room in seconds, opening the door with a surge of anticipation, the smile instantly wiped from his face when he saw his lawyer standing there.

'You're frowning. Who were you expecting?' Alec

stepped into the room, every inch the sharp lawyer, briefcase clasped in his right hand.

'No one.'

Shocked by the depths of his disappointment, Zander frowned in irritation. Why had he thought it might be her? She was on the run and there was no way she was going to turn up at his hotel room. That wasn't Lauranne's style. Far be it from her to make it easy for him.

He gritted his teeth and reflected that her stubborn resistance to the powerful attraction they shared was as infuriating as it was stimulating and that if it didn't end soon he was going to have to start conducting business meetings from a cold shower.

Alec placed his briefcase down on the table and flicked open the catches. 'Well, you were right. As usual. The old guy has agreed to a meeting.' He shook his head, admiration clearly visible in his expression. 'How do you do it? He's said no for nine months. How did you know that tonight he'd say yes?'

'Instinct.' Zander put his empty glass down and Alec smiled.

'Well, it's an instinct that's made you billions. And all that press coverage obviously worked.' Alec didn't try and hide his delight and satisfaction at the result. 'He said that for the first time he had a sense of who you really are.'

Zander almost laughed at the irony. Theo Kouropoulos had absolutely no idea who he was.

'There's just one slight complication that we hadn't anticipated—' Alec rubbed a hand over the back of his neck and Zander frowned.

'Which is?'

'He wants you to stay for ten days, to get a feel for the island and the business.' Alec swallowed. 'And he wants you to bring your—er—your wife.'

There was a long silence while Zander looked at him

thoughtfully and Alec carried on briskly. 'Obviously that's out of the question so—'

'Why is it out of the question?'

Alec gaped at him. 'Well, obviously, since you can't be in a room for five minutes without killing each other, I assumed that ten days would be an insurmountable challenge.'

'I thrive on challenge,' Zander drawled. 'I accept his invitation and ten days is fine.' *And if he had his way she wouldn't be leaving the bed for any of that time.* 'You can tell Kouropoulos that we look forward to seeing him for dinner tomorrow night.'

He smiled, pleased to have found a perfect solution to his business problem and the physical ache that had nagged him since he'd strode into Lauranne's office two weeks earlier.

He was going to sleep with her, get her out of his system and then divorce her and get on with his life.

And this time he'd make sure that there was no way she'd *forget* their relationship.

'You're going to take her with you?' Alec frowned at him, uncomprehending. 'Have you really thought this through? She probably bears you a grudge—'

'There's no probably about it.' Zander gave a wry smile as he remembered the accusations that she'd flung at him. 'She *definitely* bears me a grudge.'

Unfortunately the fact that she was fighting him every inch of the way had no significant effect on his libido.

'Then what the hell are you doing?' Alec licked dry lips, his expression nothing short of appalled. 'The last thing you should be doing is taking someone like her to the island when the negotiations are at such a delicate stage. Haven't you heard that expression about "a woman scorned"? Don't go there, Zander—you're setting yourself up for some serious confrontation. And it's going to be in public.'

Zander poured himself another whiskey, totally relaxed, a strange light flickering in his eyes. 'I thrive on confrontation.'

Alec groaned and dragged a hand through his hair. 'But not in public and not on this deal! What if she decides to take revenge on you by blowing the deal with Kouropoulos? She's hardly going to pose as a loving wife, is she?'

'That's exactly what she's going to do. Oh, and Alec—' Zander paused, a strange glitter in his dark eyes '—you can tell Kouropoulos that I want the most private villa on the complex.'

'So that she can shout abuse at you and not be heard, no doubt,' Alec muttered. 'As your lawyer I think I should be there—'

Zander gave him a smile that spoke volumes. 'Three's a crowd, Alec, and for what I have in mind I most definitely don't need a crowd.'

All he needed was one particular girl and an *extremely* large double bed.

One more night.

Lauranne adjusted the narrow straps of her red dress and looked at herself in the mirror. It was a good thing that people only saw what was on the outside, she reflected wryly. The casual observer, like the mirror, would only see the face she chose to present to the world. Composed and elegant. They would see nothing of the turmoil that raged inside her. Her battle with Zander was insignificant in comparison to the war going on inside her mind. Sense versus sexuality. Logic versus lust. Her emotions were churning around like a leaf caught in a tornado, dragged this way and that, unable to find a safe resting place.

The episode in the car had reminded her just how powerfully they connected and each clash seemed only to intensify the growing passion between them.

She lifted a finger to her glossy lips, remembering the heat and fire of his kiss. Only Zander had ever kissed her like that. And it was no wonder he'd made the assumption that they'd finish the encounter in his hotel room. She was sending out all the wrong signals. Or were they the right signals?

Totally confused about her own feelings, Lauranne slid her feet into a pair of strappy sandals and gave a wry smile. They were a pair that she loved but hardly ever wore because the heels were so high that she tended to dwarf whoever she was with.

But with Zander she needed every inch that she could muster. And there was no question of dwarfing him. It wasn't possible to dwarf Zander.

After tonight he'd be gone.

She stared at her reflection one last time. Back to Greece and out of her life. And she'd have her divorce. Which would be a good thing.

Wouldn't it?

She chewed her lip, wondering if a divorce would get rid of the pain. *The wanting.* Would she *ever* be able to respond to another man the way she responded to Zander? It was ironic that her life's passion seemed to be for a man who was as much an adversary as a lover.

The loud buzz of the intercom startled her and she took a deep breath before walking calmly to the door and opening it.

Zander stood on her doorstep, broad shoulders blocking the light, impossibly handsome in black dinner jacket.

Her first thought was that the cameras were going to have a field-day. He was just so breathtakingly good-looking that all the other men would be invisible. Her second thought was that he was smiling and she was in big trouble.

It wasn't fair of him to smile.

At least when he fought her she could fight back. When he was cold she was equally chilly. But when he smiled—

Suddenly the hostility oozed out of her and she felt hideously unsure of her own response. All she wanted to do was wrap her arms around his neck and snuggle against him,

or spend an evening in a beach-side restaurant laughing together as they attacked a plate of delicious seafood.

All she wanted was to forget the past and start again—

Shocked by her own thoughts, she tried to remind herself
that he was the enemy, but what sort of enemy made her
pulse race so frantically and made her feel so *alive?*

'I love the dress,' he said huskily, waiting for her to lock
the door and then holding out a hand. 'If I'd known I would
have driven the sports car. It matches the colour perfectly.'

She ignored the hand and arched an eyebrow, trying to
switch back to an atmosphere of attack. 'So now I'm an
accessory?'

He smiled and took her hand firmly in his, ignoring her
token resistance. 'Accessories are supposed to blend in,
agape mou. You *definitely* don't blend. You strut and lift
that pretty chin and flash your eyes at me.'

'Only when you annoy me.'

'Which is most of the time, it would seem.' His tone was
ironic and she risked a glance at him, thinking that this was
Zander at his most dangerous. The gently mocking tone, the
slightly narrowed eyes, the hint of a smile that turned his
mouth from hard to tantalisingly sexual.

It was a cruel reminder of the reasons she'd fallen in love
with him at the impressionable age of twenty-one.

They stepped into the car and instantly all her muscles
tightened with the memory of what had taken place only
hours earlier. Blood pulsed through her veins and her fingers
gripped the edge of the seat.

'Relax,' he advised softly, lounging back in the far corner
of the seat, amusement lighting his dark eyes as he registered her discomfort. 'There's no way I'm going to jump
you ten minutes before we are supposed to appear before
the general public. When you and I finally do what we're
both burning to do, we are going to have total privacy and
no deadline. And we will *not* be surrounded by paparazzi.'

Images exploded in her head and her mouth dried. 'We're not going to do anything.'

His eyes didn't leave her face. 'We're already doing it, Anni.' His voice was husky. 'This is foreplay, and you know it.'

'No—' Her denial was a soft moan that lacked conviction even to her.

He gave a slow smile. 'Actually the longest foreplay I've ever indulged in. Why do you persist in denying what we both feel?'

'Because it won't work.'

He lifted an eyebrow, his expression gently mocking. 'We've done it before, *agape mou.*' His voice was velvety smooth and utterly confident. 'We know it works.'

And that was the basic difference between them, of course. He was talking about sex. And that was all that was on offer. She turned her head and stared out of the window in a state of helpless confusion.

If she gave in to the sexual pull, where would it lead?

Ecstasy?

And then more misery.

'We're too different, Zander.'

'I'm a man and you're a woman,' he pointed out with a laugh in his voice. 'For what I have in mind, different is essential. We're *supposed* to be different.'

She turned back to him, thinking that the last thing she needed was to be reminded that he was a man. It was evident in every angle of his powerful body. Zander was masculinity in the raw. Hard where she was soft. And the woman in her responded to his strength and maleness with an eagerness that shocked her.

This was a man who had hurt her so badly that the wounds had never healed.

How could she look at him and not turn and run?

Were her instincts for self-preservation so poorly developed that she couldn't act to avoid a disaster?

But it was so much more complex than that.

Unable to analyse her own feelings, she switched the subject to business.

'So did our campaign work? Has it helped your negotiations?'

'Considerably.'

'Good.' She licked her lips, her heart banging against her ribs in response to that continued scrutiny. 'And now it's over.'

'Is it?' Something about the way he said the words made her tense but she didn't have the opportunity to question him further because at that moment the chauffeur pulled up outside the cinema and flashbulbs exploded outside the windows of the car.

Lauranne shrank back against the seat but Zander didn't flinch, his handsome face impassive as he surveyed the gathered crowds.

'Good job I didn't kiss off that lipstick,' he drawled, reaching across to take her hand. 'Smile. Publicity is your job, remember?'

'I'm not usually on this side of the camera,' she muttered, wishing that she'd volunteered someone else for this role. 'They're all going to wonder what you're doing with me.'

He gave a slow smile and shot her a look that heated the blood in her veins to boiling point. 'One look at you in that dress and they're going to know exactly what I'm doing with you, *agape mou.*'

She flushed but had no time to answer because the door opened and she stepped out onto the red carpet, smiling automatically as cameras exploded in her face.

His security team were very much in evidence but Zander seemed totally unaware of them as he slid an arm around her waist, replying to the odd shouted question with his usual cool, giving the journalists just enough but not too much.

He really didn't need her at all, she thought helplessly,

watching as he handled the assembled press with consummate ease. He knew exactly how to play the game and gave them what they wanted. No more, no less. He was the master of every situation, confident and in control at all times.

Unlike her.

Handling the media was her job, for goodness sake, but if it hadn't been for the firm grip of his fingers threaded through hers and the brush of his shoulder against her bare flesh she would have scuttled back to the car and hidden.

His hand locked tightly with hers, Zander strolled down the red carpet and then stopped, pulling her firmly against him and lowering his mouth to hers.

She gave a start of surprise but his arm slid round her and his tongue flickered into her mouth with a blatant sexuality that took the strength from her legs and the pain from her heart.

He lifted his head almost immediately, but in that brief moment Lauranne was aware only of the two of them. Flashes exploded around them in a frenzy as photographers took advantage of the photo opportunity that Zander had presented them with, but Lauranne remained oblivious.

She stared up at him, her eyes soft, her lips still damp from the intimacy of his kiss.

'Mine.' He said the word softly so that only she could hear it but there was no missing the fierce possessiveness in his tone and she felt her stomach turn over in a totally uncontrollable response.

His.

Ignoring the cameras, he smiled a smile of totally male satisfaction and then led her firmly inside the building away from flashing bulbs and curious eyes, very much the conquering Greek male.

Still stunned by the kiss, she turned to him, dazed. 'W-why did you do that?'

Why would he want to be photographed in an intimate

embrace with her when she'd spent the past two weeks trying to reshape his reputation as a womaniser?

It was asking for trouble.

Ignoring the crowds pressing against them, he pulled her against him. 'Because I didn't want any confusion.'

Shaken by the close contact, Lauranne struggled to concentrate. 'Confusion?'

'Of ownership.' He gave a self-satisfied smile and she frowned.

'I'm not one of your business deals, Zander.'

'Evidently.' He gave a sardonic smile. 'None of my business deals have ever crashed so dramatically as my relationship with you.' His hand tightened on hers and his eyes were fierce. 'But it's not going to happen again. From now on I don't share you with anyone.'

She blinked in confusion. He'd agreed to give her a divorce and here he was talking about not sharing her.

It was probably just more of his need to be in control, she decided. After all, he'd never loved her so a divorce was the inevitable outcome. But knowing Zander it would be when he decided.

'If you play the macho Greek then you know I'll fight you,' she croaked, making a feeble attempt to behave the way she felt she should and ignore her traitorous instincts.

'I expect no less.' His eyes glittered as they locked on hers. 'I love combat. Particularly when it's physical, *agape mou.*'

Suddenly breathing was a struggle. 'Zander—?'

'Have you forgotten that first time—' his voice was low and disturbingly male as he hauled her still closer to him, the hard muscle of his leg brushing against her thigh '—we were on the beach?'

He wasn't playing fair.

They should be looking forward, not back.

She closed her eyes, but it was a mistake. Without the

reality of her surroundings the images exploded in her head without restraint.

His voice was relentless. 'You'd done nothing but avoid me—'

She opened her eyes. 'You were the boss. I didn't want to get involved.'

'But I did. You were always running—' his voice purred in her ear '—teasing, playing games, making me chase you—'

Her eyes meshed with his. 'It would have been better for both of us if I'd kept running.'

A wry smile touched his firm mouth and his grip on her tightened. 'No. You were utterly sublime, *agape mou*. Not an experience I would have chosen to miss, whatever the price.'

The people around them had melted into the background. It was just the two of them. The two of them and the past.

She remembered the warmth of the sand and the weight of his powerful body as he'd neatly floored her and then rolled her under him on the beach.

'I'd never had to chase a woman before.' His smile was just for her. 'It was unbelievably erotic.'

Her breathing was shallow as she remembered what had happened afterwards.

How utterly perfect it had been—

Suddenly aware that they were the object of considerable curiosity, she chewed her lip and felt her cheeks grow hot. 'This is the wrong place for this conversation,' she muttered, mortified in case the people around them could guess what had been going on. 'Why did you ask me to come tonight?'

His eyes gleamed. 'Because I enjoy your company.'

She gave a disbelieving laugh. 'We fight.'

'I enjoy fighting,' he drawled. 'It's the reason I'm in business.'

'You're in business because you like winning.'

He smiled and reached for two glasses of champagne. 'That too.'

She looked at him in frustration. 'Have you ever lost a deal?'

'No.' He handed her one of the glasses. 'Never.'

His tone made her shiver. 'What makes you so driven, Zander?' Suddenly she wanted to understand him. 'What makes you go after more when you already have so much?'

Long dark lashes shielded the expression in his eyes. 'Because I'm a cold, ruthless businessman who doesn't have a compassionate bone in his body.'

She blushed slightly, recognising her own description. 'You never open up, do you, Zander?'

He shrugged dismissively. 'Why would I want to?'

And then people approached them, breaking the spell.

The rest of the evening passed in a haze.

Lauranne was barely aware of the film. All her senses were concentrated on the man lounging in the seat next to her. She felt the brush of his arm in the semi-darkness, the press of his knee against hers, heard the faint sound of his breathing.

She felt the connection between them so strongly that she longed to reach out and touch him but her fingers stayed still in her lap. She wasn't allowed to touch. They didn't have that sort of relationship. What they shared wasn't gentleness and giving. It was fire and flame. Heat and passion. Man and woman.

But she knew that Zander was capable of gentleness. She'd seen it in the way he'd acted towards her, felt it in the way he'd made love to her, but it was as if he resisted that side of his nature. And there had been nothing gentle about the way he'd ended their relationship.

Cold and ruthless—maybe. But what exactly had made him that way?

She sat, protected by the crowds and the darkness, contemplating what might have turned him into the man he was.

He had wealth and success, and maybe that only came to men who held themselves in isolation—who had the confidence to take risks and act without the counsel of others.

Or maybe it was something more than that.

Lost in thought, Lauranne was barely aware of the film, or of the conversation at the party afterwards. But she was very aware of Zander, standing tall and powerful by her side, cool and self-assured as he talked with various high-profile people who swarmed around him, seeking his attention.

In a room full of beautiful, powerful people Zander still dominated.

And after tonight she wouldn't see him again.

The thought was surprisingly unsettling. She should have been pleased that he was returning to Greece. Should have been relieved that the past two weeks were over.

So it came as an unpleasant shock to discover that she wasn't pleased at all.

The past two weeks had shown her that living without Zander was like existing in a power cut. She'd been stumbling round in darkness until he'd restored light to her life with a casual flick of a switch to which only he seemed to have access.

Despite everything that he'd done to her, *to them,* he'd never left her life. He'd always been there, lurking in the shadows of her mind, influencing her feelings and her decisions. The way she led her life.

Finally he slid a possessive arm around her and led her towards the waiting car.

A few hovering photographers rushed towards them but this time Zander didn't break his stride, keeping her hand clasped firmly in his as he flashed them a charismatic smile and tossed them a remark that brought instant laughter.

There wasn't a person he couldn't charm if he wanted to, she reflected helplessly as she allowed herself to be bustled into the car. He used his charm like a weapon, to be turned on when necessary.

'So—' he loosened his tie and relaxed back in his seat '—did you enjoy the film?'

For a moment she just stared at him blankly, mesmerised by the wicked smile playing around his firm mouth. She hadn't watched any of the film and he knew it.

'I—' She searched her brain for a suitably neutral answer. 'It was beautifully filmed.'

'Unbelievably tense, didn't you think?' His voice was suddenly soft and her heart started to thud.

'Y-yes.'

'And exciting—' His eyes dropped to her mouth and she knew for sure that he wasn't talking about the film.

'Zander—'

His gaze was curiously intent as he studied her mouth. 'And finally the time has come for us to stop playing games, *agape mou*.'

'Games?'

He dragged shimmering dark eyes up to hers. 'There is only so much foreplay that a guy can stand,' he said huskily, his voice impossibly sexy, 'and after the past two weeks I'm reaching that limit.'

So was she.

Which was why it was such a good thing that he was leaving. It would prevent her doing something that she'd end up regretting for the rest of her life.

Zander Volakis was like a drug. She'd kicked the habit once but now she'd had another taste the craving was stronger than ever. She needed to get away from him before she tumbled back into the abyss.

'Then perhaps it's a good job that our project is finished.'

He didn't move, his powerful frame still as he sat watching her, his dark eyes glittering with amusement and another emotion that made her heart race. 'It isn't finished.'

What did he mean, the job wasn't finished? 'We've saturated the media. There's absolutely nothing more we can do in the short term.'

'I'm not talking about the media. Thanks to the work you did, Kouropoulos is willing to meet. I'm flying out to Greece tonight.'

She stared at him, uncomprehending, wondering what his travel arrangements had to do with her. 'So you've achieved what you wanted—'

'Not quite.' His voice was soft. 'The biggest challenge is still to come. Persuading him to sell to me.'

Her heart was thumping so hard she could hardly concentrate. 'And what's that got to do with me?'

'Everything. You're going to come with me to Blue Cove Island, *agape mou*,' he said smoothly, lifting a hand and toying with a strand of blonde hair that had escaped from the pins on the back of her head. 'You're going to come as my wife, persuade Kouropoulos that I'm a warm, caring guy who can be trusted with his precious legacy. You're coming with me to Greece.'

CHAPTER SEVEN

HAVING made that announcement Zander lounged back in his seat, wondering at exactly what point he'd lost his sense of reason. His lawyer was right when he said that taking Lauranne could jeopardise the whole deal. They'd all worked long months to get to this point and he was about to put all of it at risk for a woman.

A woman who'd betrayed him.

For only the second time in his life he was at a loss to understand his own actions.

The first had been when he'd married her.

He watched through narrowed eyes as she scooted as far away from him as possible.

'There's no way I'm going with you to Greece.'

This was his chance to change his mind about taking her. This was the time for reason to prevail, but her panicked refusal simply doubled his determination to take her. Ignoring all the finely tuned instincts that had made him a billionaire by the time he was thirty, and which were now warning him that this was a mistake of monumental proportions, Zander stepped up the pressure.

'You're in my car and we're already on our way to the airport.'

'Zander, no!' Her denial was hotly passionate but he heard the shake in her voice and saw the longing in her blue eyes.

'It's a perfect opportunity to mix business with pleasure,' he said frankly, trying logic as his first approach.

'You can't possibly believe that you really need me to negotiate the deal with this K-K—'

'Kouropoulos,' Zander supplied helpfully. 'His name is Theo Kouropoulos.'

And he knew he didn't need her for the deal. Negotiating impossible deals was one of the reasons he was in business. In fact, having her there was probably the single most stupid thing he'd ever done and at the moment he didn't want to question his actions too closely.

Her eyes fixed on his. 'You promised me a divorce, Zander—'

The mere mention of their disastrous marriage should have been enough to stifle his libido but it seemed to have no effect whatsoever. Whenever he was this close to Lauranne, his brain ceased to function.

He studied her closely, noting her flushed cheeks and the hardness of her nipples pressing against the silky fabric of her dress. His body tightened in a supremely male reaction and suddenly he didn't even want to *think* about divorce. In fact he wasn't capable of thinking of *anything*. He just wanted her in his bed. 'This has nothing to do with our marriage. It has to do with the fact that we still want each other. Stop fighting me, Lauranne.'

'I want you to take me home,' she said hoarsely, her hands clasped firmly in her lap. 'Now.'

Forced to admit that logic didn't seem to be working as well as it might, Zander switched tactics with smooth efficiency, sliding along the seat so that she was forced into contact with his body.

Lifting her chin with his fingers, he stared into her eyes. 'I still want you more than I've ever wanted a woman,' he husked. 'I *burn* for you, *agape mou,* and, frankly, Kouropoulos will only have to see me with you to know that our relationship is totally genuine.'

He saw the confusion in her eyes and lowered his head, using the most effective weapon of all. Himself.

He took her mouth and felt her moan against him, her tongue flickering out to meet his as he kissed her gently.

With considerable difficulty he lifted his head so that he could continue the battle. 'What we have is *so* powerful. Why are you fighting it?'

His hand was locked in her hair and he could see a pulse beating frantically in her smooth throat.

'Because I have to.' Her voice was little more than a whisper and he could see the indecision in her eyes. 'It wouldn't work, Zander.'

'You and me on a Greek Island with no Farrer.' He gave a wry smile, watching her face. 'Trust me, Anni, it will work.'

He could read the conflict in her expression, the stubborn lift of her chin at odds with the flame in her blue eyes. She was a woman of contrasts. Soft and gentle mixed with sparky and sharp.

And he wanted her so much it was starting to drive him crazy. Lauranne was the only woman who'd ever played these games with him. Other members of her sex were prepared to fall into his bed with almost exasperating ease, but Lauranne had to fight him every inch of the way and the challenge seemed only to intensify the aching throb of his erection.

His gaze burned into hers. 'We have things to sort out, and I want to sort them out away from Farrer—'

She closed her eyes and he saw the faint colour on her cheekbones.

'Zander, please—'

'*Theos mou,* why are we playing these stupid games?' he said savagely. 'We both know what we want.'

'No!' But her denial held no conviction, the longing in her eyes at odds with the words she spoke. 'We can't do this—'

'We can,' he promised, bringing his mouth down on hers with a groan of pleasure, his tongue finding hers, tasting and teasing until she finally gave in to the fire, leaning into him, sliding her arms around his neck.

His whole body throbbed with the intensity of a desire that he had never experienced before and he dragged at the clip holding her hair, feeling it slide over his arm in a whisper of soft silk.

'*Anni—*' He'd planned to wait until they reached Greece, but suddenly the back of his car seemed increasingly appealing. He felt her slenderness, her warmth, the way she trembled against him, but just as he decided that the venue really wasn't important she pushed hard against his chest.

He shifted slightly to give her space, his hand still locked in her hair, his breathing unsteady as he stared down into her shocked, wary eyes.

'You *hurt* me, Zander.'

'You hurt me, too.' His hand tightened in her silken hair, his voice fierce. 'It's in the past.'

'I can't *do* it again.'

He saw the sheen of tears in her eyes and felt himself tense in shock.

'Anni—' He looked at her uncertainly, feeling distinctly out of his depth for the first time in his life. He'd never seen Lauranne cry before. She wasn't that sort of woman. For once all his legendary skill at negotiation deserted him.

'I *didn't* sleep with Tom!'

He gave a growl of frustration. The mere thought of her being with Tom made him want to smash something. 'I told you, it's in the past.' His tone was fierce as his eyes raked her flushed face. 'We don't mention it again.'

'But—'

'Come with me.' He didn't want to listen to her denials. He didn't want to think about it at all. 'It's what I want and it's what you want too.'

She gave a whimper and arched upwards, seeking his kiss again, but he kept himself just out of reach, gritting his teeth as he tried to ignore the extreme reaction of his body. 'If you want me, Anni, you drop this pretence and come with me. And you do it of your own free will—'

Her eyes clung to his and he watched the conflict of emotions flitting through her brain—desire, fear, confusion. He held her gaze, refusing to allow her to look away.

Her soft 'yes' was barely audible but it was the answer he wanted and he experienced the same rush of triumph that he always felt when he emerged successful from another particularly difficult negotiation.

With a groan of relief he lowered his head and kissed her soft mouth gently.

'This time it will be *so* good between us, *agape mou*—'

The touch of her mouth against his tested his self-control to intolerable levels and he pulled away with difficulty, sliding back across the seat with a rueful expression on his face.

'I have never felt so out of control with a woman,' he groaned, the admission doing very little for his ego. 'I want you all the time, everywhere, no matter how inappropriate.'

He watched the colour spill into her cheeks and the shy glance that she cast in his direction.

Anticipation throbbed between them and he gave a wry smile.

'I hope Kouropoulos isn't expecting to get much sense out of me. My main objective of going to his wretched island is to spend some time alone with you.'

The realisation that there was a strong degree of truth in that statement shocked him to an uncomfortable degree.

Suddenly something that he'd worked towards for months seemed less important and he struggled to justify such an uncharacteristic shift in his priorities. It was just sexual frustration, he brooded, coming up with the only possible answer. He'd *never* been this hot for a woman and he'd never had to wait this long for satisfaction.

And maybe there was an element of competition involved, he conceded grimly, his thoughts drifting to Farrer. It gave him considerable satisfaction to contemplate the fact that, after he'd finished with her, she wouldn't have the energy to crawl from his bed, let alone dream about Farrer.

Satisfied with that perfectly reasonable interpretation of his current state of mind, Zander pushed thoughts of his unsettling and decidedly unusual behaviour away and instead concentrated all his attentions on the woman sitting next to him.

Only *she* held the key to restoring his normal peace of mind.

She gave a hesitant smile and then reached into her tiny bag for her mobile phone. 'I'd better call Tom and tell him I won't be coming back to the office this week—'

'No.' Zander stretched out a lean brown hand and grabbed the phone from her, his expression distinctly cool. 'You can call him from Greece.'

There was no way he was allowing her to talk to Farrer before she climbed into his plane.

Fortunately he was assisted in this plan by their arrival at the airport.

He gestured outside the car. 'I don't want to keep my pilot waiting.'

He saw her eyes widen with shock. 'You were serious about the airport? But I haven't even packed any clothes—'

He resisted the temptation to point out that she wasn't going to need clothes for what he had in mind.

'I'll arrange something,' he said tactfully, urging her out of the car and into the plane with a haste that had nothing to do with his travelling schedule and everything to do with his ravenous libido.

He couldn't believe that he'd actually managed to get her this far and he was absolutely determined that nothing was going to interfere with his plans this time.

Lauranne stepped out of the car and then stopped dead, staring at the plane in front of her.

It carried the Volakis logo, another blatant reminder of just how staggeringly wealthy this man was.

What was she doing?

When they'd been together five years before she'd some-how managed to shelve the whole question of his wealth. For most of the time they'd just been two people on a beach holiday, and then for the short time they were married. But somehow she'd managed to separate Volakis the billionaire from the man she'd been crazily in love with.

'What's the matter?' He paused beside her, his dark eyes searching. And then he smiled the same smile that had eroded her resistance five years earlier. It was a smile that reassured, seduced and charmed all at the same time. A smile from which there was no escape.

She should be insisting on a divorce and heading back into London to the safety of her flat, instead of which she was willing to follow him to the moon.

He urged her up the steps and onto the plane, nodding briefly to the pretty stewardess who greeted them at the door of the aircraft.

She settled herself into one of the wide leather seats while Zander spoke a few words to his pilot and then strolled back to join her, relaxed and impossibly handsome in evening dress. He'd removed his bow-tie in the car and dark hairs clustered at the open neck of his shirt, offering a tantalising glimpse of the very male body concealed by the suit.

He sprawled in the seat next to her and she was painfully conscious of every inch of him, of the dark stubble hazing his arrogant jaw and the restless energy emanating from his powerful frame.

He wore his sexuality like a brand, a fact that obviously hadn't escaped the air stewardess, if the longing looks were anything to go by.

What was she thinking? Lauranne wondered.

She must have seen a steady stream of women pass by on Zander's arm. Perhaps she'd even been one of them.

'No. Never. Not even close.' Zander's voice was silky smooth and she turned to him in shock, her mind still else-where.

'What?'

'You were wondering whether I've ever had a relationship with her, weren't you?'

'I—I—'

He lifted a hand and stroked her blonde hair away from her face. 'The answer is never.'

'She's looking at me—' Hating herself for not playing it cool, Lauranne couldn't hide her insecurity. 'She's thinking that I'm the next one in a long line—'

He gave a wry smile. 'On the contrary, she's thinking that you're the first woman I've ever brought on this plane.'

She stared at him. 'The first woman?'

He gave a short laugh and his hand dropped to his side. 'By tomorrow the news of my deep involvement with you will be all over Greece and the international press.'

'You've never taken a woman on this plane before?'

'I can usually think of more entertaining ways of spending an evening,' he drawled, his eyes alight with amusement as he watched her face change. 'You are amazingly transparent, *agape mou*. And I love it that you're so jealous.'

'I'm not jealous.'

He smiled an infuriating smile. 'No?' The smile faded and his expression was suddenly curiously intent. 'This plane is nothing more than a convenient mode of transport. Usually I am working when I fly. It certainly isn't some sort of airborne love-nest.'

The desire to tease him overwhelmed her. 'What, never, Zander?'

His eyes gleamed in recognition of the challenge. 'Not so far. Perhaps we're about to change all that.'

Suddenly realising just how dangerous it was to tease a man like Zander, she backed off. 'I was joking.'

'So was I. For what I have in mind I definitely don't want to be in the air.' His voice was a lethal purr that stroked her nerve endings and made her shiver with anticipation. 'I think we might create a significant amount of turbulence.'

She blushed, heat flaring in her pelvis as she clashed with dark eyes glittering with a sexual promise that made her breath catch in fevered anticipation.

'Perhaps you'd better tell me something about this deal,' she said hastily. 'If I'm supposed to play a part, then you'd better brief me.'

His eyes raked her flushed cheeks and then dropped to her mouth. 'Coward.'

'Zander—'

Their eyes held for endless moments and then he gave a short laugh and relaxed back in his seat. 'The deal. What do you want to know?'

'Well, for a start, why you want to buy the island.'

There was a long silence and she felt the tension building in his powerful frame.

'Zander?' She swivelled in her seat and frowned, noting the fine lines of tension around his stunning dark eyes. 'What's wrong?'

'Nothing's wrong.' He flashed her a smile. 'And as for why I want to buy the island, it's a perfect fit for my business.'

As an answer it was both glib and plausible, but she knew instinctively that he wasn't telling her the truth.

Why did he want the island?

And why was he so tense?

She turned to look at him, her expression suddenly intent. She wanted to know. 'Talk to me, Zander. *Please.* Tell me what you're thinking.'

'I never tell anyone what I'm thinking. Now get some rest,' he advised, his tone discouraging further questioning. 'You look tired.'

And that was that.

'If I'm tired then it's your fault,' she muttered. 'I've been working ridiculously long days to give you the reputation of a saint.'

She settled down in her seat, watching as Zander flipped open his laptop and started to work on a spreadsheet.

His stamina was awesome.

She wanted to question him more but her eyelids felt heavy and she was suddenly so tired that she couldn't do anything except snuggle into her seat.

She slept soundly, waking to find that they'd landed and the sun was shining.

Groggily she struggled upright, moved the blanket that had been placed over her and looked for Zander.

He appeared from the back of the plane, freshly shaved and immaculately dressed in casual trousers and an open-necked shirt.

'You're awake.' He said something in Greek to the stewardess and then gestured towards the rear of the cabin. 'Feel free to use the bathroom to freshen up.'

Lauranne stared down at herself in dismay. 'I can't see your Kour-Kor—whatever his name is, dressed like this.'

Zander smiled. 'Then change.'

'Into what? You didn't give me time to pack, remember?'

'Select whatever you wish.'

She stared at him suspiciously and then walked to the back of the plane, pushing open a door that led to an amazingly well equipped bathroom, complete with a dressing area where several outfits hung from a rail.

Zander strolled up behind her. 'Most of our luggage is packed, but hopefully something there will meet with your approval.'

'Most of *our* luggage?'

'Of course.' He gave a casual shrug. 'If we are arriving together as a couple, then so should our luggage.'

'And if I'd refused to come?'

'Then whoever unpacked my cases would have thought that I have strange taste in clothes,' he said dryly, glancing at his watch with a frown. 'I need to make a phone call.'

Lauranne showered quickly and selected a simple linen dress in a warm shade of peach.

By the time she'd reapplied her make-up and secured her hair at the back of her head, the doors of the plane had been opened.

Zander was talking to his pilot but he broke off as she approached, his dark eyes glittering.

'Nice dress.'

She glanced down at herself self-consciously. 'It fits really well. How did you know my size?'

He gave a wicked smile. 'That is not a question to ask me in public, *agape mou.*' He nodded to his pilot and stood to one side so that she could walk down the steps.

Even though it was still early, the heat made her gasp and she reached inside her bag for a pair of sunglasses.

Zander took her arm and led her towards the waiting car.

'Certainly beats airport terminal buildings,' Lauranne muttered as she slid into the sumptuous interior.

'This island has a tiny airstrip,' he informed her, settling himself next to her. 'Kouropoulos built it only two years ago. Before that you had to take a boat from the nearest island with a runway if you wanted to stay here.'

'It must have been nice like that,' she said wistfully, staring out of the window at the passing landscape. 'Sort of undeveloped and hard to get to.'

He shot her a look that she couldn't interpret. 'It was extremely underdeveloped before Theo Kouropoulos took over.'

'Did you know it before then?'

He tensed and thick dark lashes shielded his expression. 'I visited here as a child.'

She looked at him, sensing there was a great deal more than he was saying. 'On holiday?'

His hesitation was so brief it was barely perceptible. 'Yes. On holiday.'

She watched him for a moment and then turned her head,

gasping with delight as the road curved upwards, revealing tiny bays glistening in the morning sun.

'The beaches are stunning.'

'Most of them are only accessible by boat,' he told her, leaning across so that he could see what she was admiring. 'It reduces its appeal as a tourist resort.'

'Kouropoulos obviously didn't think so?'

'He built his resort on the south of the island,' Zander said flatly. 'It has several pretty, sandy beaches, perfect for safe bathing and water sports. The rest of the island is now uninhabited.'

She eyed him sideways. 'Where did you used to stay?'

His broad shoulders tensed. 'I beg your pardon?'

'When you were a child,' she prompted him gently. 'Where did you stay when you came here as a child?'

He sucked in a breath. 'In a house—'

'Right.' As answers went it was economical to say the least, but Lauranne knew better than to push. Sharing personal information about himself wasn't one of Zander's strong points. She watched him for a moment but his handsome face was as inscrutable as ever. For a man who was so intensely physical, he was ridiculously repressed when it came to expressing other emotions.

Wondering whether his childhood holidays had anything to do with his desire to possess the island, Lauranne turned her attention back to the view, peering out of the window as the road curved again and started moving downwards.

Below she could see whitewashed buildings and curved swimming pools.

'That's it. Blue Cove Resort.'

Sensing his tension, she instinctively reached out a hand and took his, squeezing it gently. 'I've never seen you stressed about business. Don't worry, between us we'll convince him to sell.'

His glance reflected his surprise and she managed a smile,

feeling pretty surprised herself. When had she stopped fighting him and turned supportive?

The driver pulled into a driveway and said something in Greek.

'We're here.' Zander gently disengaged his hand. 'Now don't forget, you're so in love with me you can't see straight.'

Her heart flipped over. Five years earlier that would have been a perfect description of the way she'd felt about him.

And now?

She swallowed, totally confused about her feelings. She couldn't think straight when he was near and she couldn't breathe properly either.

All she knew was that she had to be with him.

Zander was shaking hands with an older man who immediately strode towards her with a smile on his face.

'And you must be Lauranne! I must admit the cameras don't do you justice!'

'Cameras?' Lauranne looked at him in confusion and then glanced at Zander for enlightenment. 'What cameras?'

'Your picture is in every newspaper,' Kouropoulos told her with a smile. 'Volakis reuniting with his beautiful wife is the top story. Did you enjoy the film?'

Lauranne froze as she realised what must have happened. That kiss—

'The film was very enjoyable,' she said stiffly, hiding her growing anger with difficulty.

Just exactly at what point had she become such a gullible fool that she'd believed that Zander wanted her with him for her charms? Business always came first with Zander, and this was obviously no exception.

He'd used her—

Kouropoulos gave her a searching look. 'You look a little pale. You must be tired. In which case I hope my next piece of news will be welcome. I'm afraid I have to fly to Athens this afternoon to deal with an urgent business issue. I won't be back until Friday. We can start our negotiations then. In the meantime I'll arrange for someone to show you to your villa straight away and you can relax. There is a boat at your disposal so that you can explore some of the bays.'

Zander inclined his dark head and Lauranne gritted her teeth, afraid to say anything at all in case she exploded. She was still too angry by the realisation that she'd been manipulated to react to the news that she and Zander were expected to entertain themselves for almost a week before they even had a meeting with Kouropoulos.

She fumed silently as they were driven through the resort, barely aware of the sumptuousness of her surroundings. The resort consisted of individual whitewashed villas, each with its own pool and shady terrace with a fabulous view of the sea. In normal circumstances Lauranne would have been enchanted, but these were not normal circumstances. She was so upset and angry with Zander that she was simmering with suppressed rage, totally unable to relax. She couldn't *believe* that she'd fallen for his charm again. All that rubbish about wanting to be with her when all the time he was just manipulating the situation so that he could gain control of his precious island.

Evidently aware that something was amiss, he cast her a searching look, but before he could speak they arrived at their own villa, set in a secluded position at the edge of the resort.

Fabulous for a honeymoon, Lauranne thought, grinding her teeth as she marched up the little path to the front door, her chin and shoulders set for battle.

Once they were safely inside the villa and the door had closed behind the staff member who'd accompanied them, she turned on Zander, eyes flashing, totally oblivious to the extreme luxury of the interior of the villa.

'So *that's* why you kissed me!' She was so angry and hurt she thought she'd burst. 'You did it for the cameras! So that Kouropoulos would wake up to a photo of us both.

Husband reunited with wife. It was just another trick to convince him that you're a caring, compassionate guy whereas actually you're a devious, manipulative—'

'It's business.' Zander interrupted her sharply, a frown touching his dark brows. 'It doesn't change the way I feel about you. Calm down. Someone might hear you yelling.'

She glared at him, so hurt that she wanted to commit bodily harm. 'And blow the cover that you so carefully prepared—'

'You're being ridiculous,' he gritted. 'What have you been doing for the past two weeks if it wasn't manipulating the press?'

'That's different.' She sighed, numb inside. How could she have fallen for his patter? How could she have believed that he truly wanted her? 'You show no respect for me. You may be a billionaire and used to having your own way in everything, but I won't be one of your toys, Zander, to be discarded when you've had enough.'

'Toys?' He looked at her with grim amusement. 'Toys are straightforward and give only pleasure. Handling you requires a qualification in bomb disposal. Believe me, *agape mou,* if I was after a light-hearted diversion I wouldn't be with someone who starts a battle every time we're alone.'

'You used me!'

'I was extending what you'd already done,' he shot back. 'You wanted the public to take away a certain message and so did I.'

'That we're involved.' She virtually spat the words and he frowned.

'We are involved.'

'No.'

'Yes, we are. The picture spoke the truth. It has no bearing on our relationship.'

'You *used* me.' Her eyes sparkled with the tears she was struggling to hold back and her breathing was jerky. 'Why did you bring me here, Zander? There are plenty of women out there who would have loved to come with you. Who would have fallen over themselves to pretend to be in love with you. Why pick me? I *hate* you—'

'No, you don't.' He contradicted her smoothly. 'You want to hate me but you can't, just as I can't hate you. And I picked you because I can't keep my hands off you.'

Her heart rate doubled and she dug her nails in her palms, reminding herself of what he'd just done. 'You kissed me for the cameras.'

Even to her own ears she sounded like a sulky child and she almost groaned as Zander gave an all-male chuckle.

'I kissed you because you looked delectable, *agape mou,*' he said softly, closing the distance between them and sliding a long finger under her chin. 'Look at me.'

She resisted at first but the relentless pressure of his finger increased until she was forced to look at him. He slid his other arm around her hips and pulled her firmly against him.

She gasped as she felt the thickness of his erection through the thin fabric of her dress.

'Zander—'

'You think I manufacture this for the cameras?'

He gave a rueful smile and she fell headlong into the charm of that smile with a catch of her breath.

'You're a louse—'

He slid a hand round her cheek and ran his thumb over her soft mouth. 'I *refuse* to fight with you—'

Her tongue flickered out and touched his thumb and their eyes locked for endless seconds while the tension grew, tension that had been building steadily for the two weeks they'd been together.

They cracked at the same moment.

With a violent curse Zander crashed his mouth down on hers just as she rose on tiptoe, her hands locked in the front of his shirt, dragging him towards her.

It was a bruising, brutal, desperate kiss that was the result of weeks of denial.

He grasped her head in his hands, his strong fingers biting into her scalp as he held her fast. His kiss was dark and dangerous, rough and raw, and her mouth opened under the burning heat of his, welcoming the fire.

Without releasing her head, he pushed her back against the door, flattening her body with his. He ground his hips hard against her and she sobbed his name against his mouth, squirming against the blatant evidence of his arousal.

He lifted her in one strong movement, jerking up her dress and crashing her back against the door, supporting her easily with his powerful body.

She shifted against him, struggling to relieve the throb in her pelvis, and he swore and anchored her with strong hands, his movements sure and skilful as he tore the delicate silk of her panties.

She arched in anticipation, but he held her firmly, his first thrust so shockingly hard and hot that she cried out in shock and relief, the sound mingling with his kiss.

It was sex at its most basic, a splintering, blistering animal mating, so physically intense that it was beyond the scope of human description. It was fast and hard and utterly primitive, each thrust so deep that she sobbed aloud with agonising pleasure.

Her eyes closed and he dragged his mouth away from hers, his breathing laboured as he joined them in the most intimate way possible.

'Look at me, Anni—' His hoarse command penetrated her brain and her eyes flew open, connecting with the blaze in his. '*Look at me.*'

So she did and he possessed every single part of her as he drove them both to the ultimate satisfaction.

Sensation ripped through her and her climax hit so hard that she cried out in disbelief, her nails digging into his shoulders as her body convulsed around his. He swore and thrust hard, his body erupting into hers with hot, liquid force and she clung to him, unable to draw breath, suspended at another level until gradually the contractions faded and she went limp in his arms.

He closed his eyes briefly and then gently he withdrew and lowered her to the ground, stifling her soft gasp with his mouth.

'God, Anni—' His arms were still round her, holding her against him, supporting her when her own legs wouldn't.

Her face was buried in his chest, breathing in his male smell, feeling the dampness of his flesh against her burning cheeks. He was all hard muscle and throbbing masculinity and she closed her eyes tightly, struggling with the reality of what they'd just shared.

She didn't want to speak.

Speaking just had to spoil it.

And maybe he felt it too, because he swung her off her feet and into his arms, and strode through to the bedroom, his mouth tightly shut.

He lowered her onto the bed and came down over her, his breathing still unsteady as he stared down into her flushed, shocked face.

'That was *not* for the cameras.'

She managed a weak smile. 'I should hope not or your reputation will be shot to pieces for ever.'

He didn't laugh, his face grimly serious as he stroked her tangled blonde hair away from her face.

'I have *never* wanted a woman the way I want you. It scares me.'

She froze, stunned into silence by that uncharacteristically emotional admission.

'I pride myself on my self-control, but with you—' he broke off, lowering his mouth to the pulse in her throat like a man who couldn't help himself '—with you I'm just so *desperate* I don't know myself.'

It was the nearest he'd ever come to suggesting that what they shared was special and she held her breath, wanting him to say more. Wanting him to reveal something of his feelings.

'Zander—'

She felt the hot, teasing lick of his tongue against her skin and the immediate response of her own body and then he lifted his head, his eyes glittering as he stared down at her. 'For two weeks I've watched you, wanting to rip off every scrap of clothing and have you under me. I thought I was going mad—'

Lauranne stared at him with helpless frustration, realising that he'd managed to reduce their relationship to just sex once again. And having done that he seemed suddenly energised, the brooding introspection so fleeting that it might never have happened.

Having rationalised his feelings to his satisfaction, he sat up and ripped off his shirt, exposing his powerful chest.

Deciding that if just sex was all that was on offer then she'd make the most of it, Lauranne lifted a hand, her fingers tangling with the dark curls that covered the perfect musculature.

He caught her hand in his and lifted it to his mouth, his eyes still locked with hers as he licked her fingers suggestively before sucking them into the heat of his mouth.

Her body throbbed in response and her hips shifted on the bed, her dress riding up to her waist. With a rough groan he raised her up, dealt with her zip and stripped her naked in less time than it took to gasp out his name. Then he threw off the last of his own clothes and came down onto the bed next to her, lithe, handsome and shockingly male.

Her eyes skimmed over him and she felt the sparks of excitement shooting through her hopelessly aroused body. The sexual attraction between them was so breathtakingly powerful that she knew there was absolutely no hope for her. He was magnificent in every way, perfectly proportioned and indecently good-looking.

He kissed his way down her body with a gratifying

amount of male appreciation, muttering something in Greek as his mouth found the soft swell of her breasts.

Shaping her with his strong hands, he licked at her nipple with skilled strokes of his tongue, sending powerful darts of sensation coursing through her helplessly trembling body. Then he slid down her body and what happened next was the most shockingly exciting experience of her life. She squirmed and writhed under the touch of his clever mouth, her fingers curling into the sheets as her whole body simmered with a sexual need so strong that it threatened to engulf her.

She felt so frantic that she didn't recognise herself and she wanted him so badly that she was willing to *beg*. Finally, when she'd given up and decided that she was definitely going to die of pleasure, he slid back up her body and parted her thighs.

'You are so sexy, *agape mou*,' he husked, simmering dark eyes raking her flushed face with a gratifying degree of male appreciation. 'And I love the way that you want me as much as I want you—'

Without giving her a chance to reply, he thrust smoothly inside her wildly excited body, trapping her cries of pleasure with his mouth.

She moved against him, desperate to cool the burning fire in her pelvis, aching to reach the fulfilment that only he could give her. But he slowed the pace, thrusting hard and deep, driving her higher and higher until she experienced a climax so explosive that she dug her nails in his back and sobbed his name.

She felt him shudder against her, felt his hard, powerful body deep inside hers and then he rolled onto his back, taking her with him, her damp, breathless body held firmly against his.

And then she knew—

Lying in his arms, she knew without a doubt that she loved him and she always had. That was the reason she'd married him, even though she'd always known that he didn't love her.

And that was the reason she hadn't divorced him.

Because she hadn't been able to. In her heart she would always be married to Zander.

Depressed by the knowledge that she could never enjoy a casual relationship with him, she lay still, coming to terms with the painful realisation that she was heading for a major emotional disaster again.

'So now are you convinced that I want you?' he drawled softly, stroking her tangled hair away from her flushed face.

Lauranne closed her eyes, shaken to the core by the intensity of the experience they'd just shared.

She *knew* he wanted her, but she wanted it to be more than that—

So much more than that.

Determined not to dwell on the impossible, she snuggled closer to him and closed her eyes, making the most of the moment.

For a brief second she felt him tense and braced herself for rejection but surprisingly he didn't push her away. Instead he hesitated briefly and then dropped a kiss on her damp forehead.

'That was *utterly* incredible,' he groaned hoarsely. 'The best sex I've ever had.'

The best sex—

His words collided uncomfortably with the soppy thoughts she'd been having, but she pushed them away and snuggled closer still, trying to ignore his slight resistance to her affection.

Too tired and sated after his passionate lovemaking to worry about the future, Lauranne felt her eyes drift closed and decided that cuddling Zander was absolutely her favourite way in the world to fall asleep.

As her soft body curled trustingly around his, Zander lay stiff as a board trying to work out what was happening to him. As a Greek who prided himself on his self-control, he was uncomfortably aware that he'd been displaying very little of it since the day he'd walked into Lauranne's London office.

Telling himself that the only reason he wasn't pushing her away was because he didn't want to wake her up when she was clearly very tired, he stared up at the ceiling and tried to make some sense of the situation.

Bringing her to the island had *not* been a good idea, he admitted, struggling to explain to himself exactly what had prompted such an uncharacteristically impulsive decision. He was taking a ridiculous and unnecessary risk. She was totally capable of blowing the whole deal for him.

Forced to concede that for the first time in his life his libido had been involved in a business decision, he consoled himself with the thought that it was perfectly natural for a red-blooded male to be occasionally distracted by an exceptionally beautiful woman.

And Lauranne was exceptionally beautiful. And spirited. And clever. And interesting. As the list of her qualities grew alarmingly long, Zander switched tack and concentrated hard on her down points.

After several long frustrating minutes during which all he managed to come up with was the fact that she'd been the one to end their relationship five years before, he decided that maybe that was the key to his current behaviour.

Accustomed to being the one in the driving seat, he'd *always* been the one to decide when a relationship ended. Which made his current obsession the result of a perfectly understandable masculine desire to be in control. And on top of that the sex was mind-blowing and, as he was a normal male with a healthy appetite in that direction, it was perfectly natural to seek every opportunity to enjoy what was on offer.

But despite his attempts to rationalise his behaviour a

tiny, nagging portion of his mind kept reminding him that, no matter how good the sex in previous relationships, he'd *always* managed to make it to the bed before seducing a woman. With Lauranne he'd barely managed to close the door behind them before subjecting them both to the hottest, most elemental sexual encounter he'd ever experienced.

What the hell was happening to him?

She gave a little moan in her sleep and rolled away from him and Zander waited for the feeling of relief that always came once the necessary post-coital affection was over. Instead he found himself fighting an alien impulse to drag her back against him.

Utterly discomforted by the direction of his own thoughts, he sprang out of bed with a fluent curse and made his way to the shower, turning the setting to cold.

The simplest solution to all this was to get her out of his system as fast as possible, he decided, gritting his teeth as needles of freezing water cooled his decidedly overheated body.

After all, he'd successfully worked every other female of his acquaintance out of his system with remarkably little problem.

Why should Lauranne be different?

Sex and then divorce. No problem. He absolutely *wasn't* developing feelings for her.

Lauranne awoke to find Zander fully dressed and watching her as if she were an extremely dangerous and unpredictable animal.

'Great. You're awake.' He spoke with a disturbing degree of brisk detachment given the intimacies they'd shared only an hour earlier. 'Now we can go for a walk.'

A *walk?*

Still groggy with sleep, the pleasurable ache of her body reminding her of the intensity of their lovemaking, Lauranne struggled valiantly to understand his sudden change in focus.

Had she imagined it, or had she fallen asleep curled in his arms?

Just exactly at what point had he managed to rise, shower and dress without her noticing? And why was he now looking at her as though she was the biggest mistake he'd ever made in his life?

A *walk*?

She sat up in bed and he sucked in a breath and took a step backwards, almost tripping over in his attempt to put distance between them.

Wondering what on earth the problem was, Lauranne frowned at him in confusion.

'Why don't you come back to bed?'

But Zander shook his head and backed towards the door, fumbled with the handle and exited onto the terrace with an undignified degree of haste.

Totally at a loss to understand his strange reaction, she took a deep breath and slid out of bed, dressing quickly and reaching for a pretty sun hat that she'd found in her luggage. If he wanted to walk, then they'd walk.

He'd obviously gone totally mad.

Opening the door, she paused for a moment, her eyes on those powerful shoulders as he stood with his back to her, staring down at the beach with an ominous frown on his handsome face.

Hearing her behind him, he turned and she felt her heart bang against her ribs as she collided with those amazingly sexy dark eyes.

She ought to be running a mile, she thought helplessly as she floundered and drowned in the intensity of his gaze. She was an intelligent woman and she knew he was *never* going to change. So why was she still standing in front of him?

Closing the door behind her, she walked up to him, waiting for him to back away again.

But he didn't back away.

Instead he hesitated briefly and then caught her against him and kissed her as if he couldn't help himself and then dragged his mouth away from hers with a savage curse. 'Two weeks without sex is an *extraordinarily* long time, *agape mou*—'

She stared at him dizzily, still reeling from his possessive kiss and wondering why he was trying to find excuses for kissing her. She was just relieved and flattered that he found her so irresistible physically. It was obviously all she could expect of him and she was determined to make the most of it.

'Are you ready?' Back to his supremely confident self, he threw her a sizzling smile. 'I want to show you my island.'

'You haven't bought it yet,' she reminded him and he flashed her a smile.

'But I will.'

'It doesn't cross your mind that you might fail, does it?'

He looked amused, evidently considering her question to be totally superfluous. 'No. It doesn't. Come on. We're going exploring.'

'Do I bring a swimming costume?'

His eyes gleamed with masculine intent 'Depends on how brave you're feeling.'

They strolled out of the villa and he hesitated and then took her hand firmly in his, adjusting his long stride so that she could more easily keep pace with him.

Trying not to read anything into that touch, she forced a casual smile. 'Where's the photographer this time, Zander?'

He frowned briefly. 'Can't a guy be romantic?'

'Yes, but you don't *do* romantic, Zander.'

He looked taken aback, his grip on her hand tightening. 'What have we been doing since we arrived at the villa?'

'That was just sex,' she said flatly and something flared in his eyes.

'There's no *just* about it. What we share is *so* good and I love the fact you don't demand the emotional pretence that often goes with a physical relationship.'

Rendered speechless by his total lack of ability to appreciate the true extent of her feelings, Lauranne failed to manage anything in the way of a response. Stunned into silence, she reminded herself that if she *ever* managed to get through this and fall in love again then it was going to be with a man who was in touch with his emotions.

Zander was not only severely allergic to *her* emotions, but he evidently didn't want to make even a passing acquaintance with his own either.

Finally she found her voice. 'Emotional pretence?'

Zander shrugged. 'My father was continually confusing sex with love,' he drawled, 'and it was a mistake that cost him a fortune.'

Still reeling from his blind rejection of even the slightest degree of emotion on her part, Lauranne looked at him blankly. 'Your father?' Zander had never discussed his family with her before. And he'd certainly never mentioned his father. 'What about your father?'

Zander frowned. 'He *never* learned. One expensive divorce settlement should have been enough to inject him with a healthy degree of cynicism about women, but it didn't. Every time he met a new woman he thought he was in love and he just gave them everything they wanted.'

'Oh!' Lauranne considered this statement thoughtfully. 'I suppose if you're seriously rich then it is sensible to show a little more caution in relationships, but I like the fact that he approached each one with optimism. Now that *is* romantic.'

'Romantic?' Zander stopped dead and threw her an incredulous look, the stunned look in his dark eyes almost comical. 'What's romantic about being taken for a ride?'

'But he started each relationship believing that it would last,' Lauranne breathed, her eyes slightly misty as she contemplated the trusting nature of a man that she'd never even met. 'Is he happily married now?'

'He died,' Zander said flatly, 'when I was twenty-one, leaving behind him a mountain of debts, a large number of extremely disgruntled employees and investors and some *very* rich, smug women.'

Lauranne bit her lip, stunned by the revelation and experiencing for the first time a small insight into the complex workings of Zander's character.

Suddenly she had a brief glimpse of what might have made him the man he was.

'I really wanted you to tell me that eventually he met someone lovely who was worthy of him.' She touched his arm. 'I'm sorry. That must have been so hard for you.'

'Well, let's just say I learned a valuable lesson early in life,' he drawled, a sardonic smile on his handsome face. 'That love comes with a high price tag.'

Lauranne wondered how his remark could cause so much pain when she *knew* that he didn't love her.

'Only you could produce a balance sheet for a relationship,' she said lightly and he shrugged.

'Had my father done the same then he might not have lost everything.'

'What about your mother?' Lauranne held her breath as she waited for the answer, but he merely shrugged, showing not one flicker of emotion on his face.

'My mother was wife number two. She stayed around long enough to give him me, and then she decided to use my father's generosity to fund her less savoury lifestyle.'

Lauranne winced. 'That's awful—'

He shot her an impatient look. '*Don't* start performing amateur psychology on me, *agape mou*. I don't even remember her, so I can hardly blame her for my shortcomings.'

But she had to be at least part of the reason that he was so emotionally detached, Lauranne reasoned, struggling to keep pace with him as he lengthened his stride along the path that led to the beach.

Deciding that the time had come to change the subject, she cast him a wary look. 'Are you angry that Kouropoulos invited you here and then vanished?'

Zander laughed. 'He is playing games, Lauranne. And no, I'm not angry. I'm relieved. It will be nice to have some time together, just the two of us.'

She swallowed, refusing to allow herself to read anything into that comment. He was talking about sex again, nothing else.

They walked across the beach and then onto a narrow path that led away from the beach and she suddenly realised that he was walking with a sense of purpose and direction.

'Where are we going?'

For a moment she thought he wasn't going to answer her. 'There's something I want to see.'

The path climbed upwards and soon Lauranne was breathless in the heat. 'Slow down.'

He stopped immediately and shot her a rueful smile. 'I'm sorry— I wasn't thinking. We're here.'

Where was here?

He slowed his pace and the path curved to the right and suddenly she found herself staring down at a perfect crescent-shaped beach. The soft golden sand curved in an arc around a clear blue sea.

'Oh.' Lauranne stopped dead in surprise and delight. 'It's totally idyllic. So gorgeous. Like something out of a travel brochure.'

Next to her Zander was silent, a strange look in his dark eyes. 'Yes.' His voice was slightly roughened and she sensed a tension in him that hadn't been there before. 'It's called Blue Cove Beach because the colours are so intense. The island is named for this beach.'

'I've never seen anywhere so lovely. And look at the

house.' She gazed in awe. 'What a fantastic position. I wonder if anyone lives there now.'

'No one lives there.'

Something about his tone made her hold her breath. 'But they used to?'

'Many years ago.'

And then she remembered what he'd said in the car. 'This is it, isn't it? The house you used to stay in as a child—' It was a wild guess but the instant tension in his powerful frame told her that she was right.

He didn't speak, a strange look glittering in his dark eyes as he stared at the pretty whitewashed house.

The silence stretched and stretched and Lauranne held herself still, feeling as though she was intruding on something intensely private.

'That's why you want the island, isn't it?' She spoke softly, as if whispering would give him the choice of ignoring her words. 'That house is the reason.'

A muscle flickered in his rough jaw. 'Yes.'

She bit her lip and glanced first at him and then at the house. 'Do you want to go down there? To the beach?'

The change in him was barely perceptible but she sensed his indecision. 'No. Not today.'

Lauranne looked at the house again and then took his hand. It was a gesture of comfort, of closeness, and for a tense moment she wondered whether he'd reject her. Reminding herself that what they shared was physical not emotional, she braced herself for the inevitable withdrawal on his part.

But it didn't come.

After a brief hesitation his fingers tightened on hers, locking her against him.

'Who lived there, Zander?'

She thought he wasn't going to answer her and then he inhaled sharply, his eyes fixed on the house. 'My grandmother. She lived here all her life.'

'The house belonged to her?'

'The whole island belonged to my father, but he lost it in a divorce settlement,' Zander said harshly, and then he turned and started walking back along the path without uttering another word.

The fact that he kept an almost painful grip on her hand gave her a flicker of hope. At this moment in time he *needed* her, and for something other than sex. The fact that he'd shared even a tiny bit of what was in his mind felt like an enormous step forward. She felt as though she'd managed to open the door to his mind just a crack and been rewarded with a tantalising peep of what lay inside.

Why had they never once discussed his background before? Why had he kept so much of himself a secret from her?

It occurred to her that she'd never really known him at all.

'Did your grandmother lose her home?'

He slowed his pace and shook his head, his expression bleak. 'She would have done, but in the event she died before she was forced to move out.'

Lauranne stopped dead, shocked and distressed by his bald statement. 'No!'

'She was devastated that my father had lost the island.' Zander stared at the sea, his eyes fierce. 'She was very elderly and she *never* got over the shock.'

Lauranne tried to imagine what it must be like to lose the home that you'd lived in all your life.

'That's terrible—'

'I was staying with her when she died. I found her.' His tone was matter-of-fact but Lauranne still had her hand in his and she felt the sudden painful tightening of his fingers on hers. 'I was nine years old.'

Without thinking, Lauranne stepped forward and slid both her arms around him, feeling his pain so acutely that the tears welled up and spilled down her cheeks. 'That's so awful—'

His mouth twisted but his arms tightened around her. 'What was awful was losing the only person who actually bothered about me,' he confessed. 'And she was so angry with my father. The night before she died she made me promise that I'd get the island back.'

Lauranne closed her eyes, finally understanding what this was all about.

He was fulfilling his promise.

The promise of a nine-year-old boy to his beloved grandmother.

The knowledge choked her. 'So has Kouropoulos always owned it?'

Zander shrugged. 'Virtually. It was sold to him by wife number three. He's owned it for twenty-six years and up until now he's always refused to sell.'

'So what makes you think he'll sell now?'

'He's in financial difficulty.' Zander frowned. 'To be honest I'm mystified as to why he hasn't sold sooner.'

'Does he know why you want it?'

Zander shrugged. 'I have no idea.'

'Your father must have been devastated to lose it.'

'He had bigger problems to worry about. His entire company was going under,' Zander said. 'When he died the company was in a mess.'

Lauranne looked at him. 'It must have been so hard for you.'

'I was thrown in the deep end,' Zander admitted, his handsome face blank of expression. 'The company had been struggling for the best part of a decade. There were thousands of employees relying on me for jobs. My entire focus was on turning the company around as fast as possible.'

He obviously felt an enormous sense of responsibility for his employees and she frowned slightly, remembering how everyone had sung his praises during the interviews she'd arranged with the media.

Without exception, the people who worked for him seemed to think he was a very good boss.

'And you did turn it around.' And he'd done it at a ridiculously young age. 'How did you do it? How did you build the company into what it is today?'

'By being ruthless, cold and unemotional, *agape mou*.' His eyes gleamed as he quoted her again and she gave a rueful smile, fascinated and warmed by the new insight into his character.

He wasn't unemotional. She knew that now. In fact she'd seen more emotion in him during the past hour than in all the rest of the time they'd been together. There was no doubting his fierce love for his grandmother, the hurt caused by his father and his loyalty towards those who worked for him. He certainly wasn't unemotional and if he'd been cold and ruthless then maybe it had been because he'd had so much responsibility thrust on him at a young age. With no support from family.

'When your mother left, who did you live with?'

He gave a humourless laugh. 'The next wife. And you should probably feel sorry for them rather than me,' he drawled, lifting a hand to ward off sympathy. 'I was the child from hell. I think I was personally responsible for wife number four leaving.'

'No child would have been able to do that if she'd truly loved your father.' She hesitated. 'Your childhood must have been very lonely. Is that the reason you give so much money to children's charities?'

'My childhood was fine.' His tone was slightly chilly, discouraging any further exploration down that route. 'I learned at an early age to rely on no one but myself and that has been the best business lesson of all.'

Lauranne bit her lip.

It might have benefited his business, but it had done nothing for his ability to trust women.

He really, really didn't believe in love and she was beginning to understand why.

What the hell was the matter with him?

Zander ground his teeth in irritation. He *never* spilled his guts to *anyone,* and here he was talking to Lauranne about subjects that he had never discussed with another living soul.

The touch of her fingers on his arm and the sympathy in her blue eyes had eroded the emotional barriers he'd built between himself and the world.

Stunned by his own uncharacteristic behaviour, he ignored the concerned look in her eyes and strode ahead towards the crowded beach, trying to drag his mind back to a state that he recognised.

What was it that she did to him?

Why did he always behave in a manner that was totally out of character whenever he was near her?

Lauranne flashed him a smile and lifted her face to the sun. 'Fancy a paddle before dinner?'

'A *paddle?*' Thrown by the change of subject, he threw back his head and laughed, some of the tension leaving him. 'You sound about six years old.'

Only she didn't look six years old.

She was a full woman and keeping his hands off her was becoming more difficult by the minute.

'Maybe, but everyone should behave like a child once in a while,' Lauranne told him, slipping off her shoes and running towards the water shrieking with laughter as he grabbed her from behind and almost toppled her in. 'You rat!'

He swung her into his arms, a wicked expression in his eyes. 'What will you give me not to drop you?'

'I'll give you a black eye if you *do* drop me.' Her arms

were round his neck and he held her easily. 'Try explaining that to Theo Kouropoulos.'

He waded slightly deeper. 'I'm beginning to wish that Theo Kouropoulos and his whole damn resort would just vanish,' he muttered, his Greek accent suddenly very pronounced. 'I want to make love to you on a beach and I would far rather we didn't have an audience.'

He felt her tremble in his arms. 'Do you remember the Caribbean?'

He gave a groan and shot her a reproachful look. 'You ask me that here? In such a public place? Have you no mercy?'

'It was just you and me,' she said softly, her tongue flicking out to moisten her lips, 'with the dark as curtains and the swish of the sea on the sand.'

He muttered something in Greek and dropped her in the water.

With a yelp of laughter she landed on her feet, clutching at his shirt. 'What are you doing?'

'Cooling us both down.' He shot her a sizzling smile and splashed water in her direction.

'Zander! Stop it!'

'I thought you wanted to behave like a child.'

She was still laughing as she wiped the sea water from her eyes, but as she met the burn of his dark gaze there was nothing of the child in her eyes.

Before she could speak, he grabbed her wrist in his fingers and virtually dragged her through the water and back to the sand, pausing briefly to pick up their shoes before striding purposefully back towards their villa.

Lauranne shot him a glance and her heart turned over as she read the blatant intent in his eyes.

Inside the villa he kicked the door shut behind him and brought his mouth down on hers with a ferocity that made her gasp in ecstasy.

Without a second's hesitation he relieved her of her dress and dealt with her silk panties with similar speed.

Breathing heavily, their mouths clashed again in a wild, frantic kiss, tongues tangling, breath mingling as they attacked each other with the passion that characterised their whole relationship.

With a swift movement he kicked off his own shorts and lowered her to the floor.

She gasped as the cool marble touched her skin and then cried out as she felt his fingers slide between her thighs.

'Zander—'

'You're so wet for me already,' he said thickly, shifting her under him and entering her with a hard thrust that made her sob with pleasure. He plunged into her with an expert rhythm, the slick, heated glide of his flesh inside and against hers driving her skywards.

It was so fast and intense that when it was over Lauranne lay in shock, unable to believe what she'd just done.

Zander obviously felt the same way.

'Remind me to tell Kouropoulos that he needs to redesign these villas,' he groaned, wincing as he rolled onto his back. 'Marble is *not* very comfortable.'

'The bedroom was only a few metres away,' she pointed out huskily and he pulled a face.

'Too far. I wanted you on the beach. This was a compromise.'

As her breathing slowed she rolled to face him, 'Are you injured? I could give you the kiss of life.' She grinned mischievously and he groaned.

'No, don't touch me, you witch!' He sprang to his feet and dragged her with him. 'We're going to spend the afternoon in the pool. Cold water should do the trick.'

Privately Lauranne thought it was going to take a great deal more than cold water to subdue the way she felt about him, but she was careful not to share those thoughts.

Instead she walked through to the bedroom, changed into a bikini, and met him by the pool.

'This is gorgeous.' The pool was a perfect oval of tempting blue, totally private and surrounded by colourful pots of geraniums. 'Do all the villas have their own pools?'

Zander nodded. 'I think so. Kouropoulos developed this bit of the island as an up-market resort for families. Each villa is state-of-the-art in terms of design and equipment. There are several private beaches, water sports and nannies to look after the children. Basically all the ingredients for a perfect family holiday.'

Lauranne sat on the edge of the pool and dipped her toes in the water. 'Mmm. That feels so nice.' Her smile faltered slightly as she glanced up and saw him stripping down to a pair of swimming trunks. Deciding that a swim was called for, she slid into the water and swam to the other side of the pool.

Zander dived in and caught up with her, crossing the pool in powerful strokes, his handsome face glistening with water as he surfaced next to her.

He dragged her against him and she felt the heat of his body contrasting with the cool of the water.

Hating herself for being so responsive to him, Lauranne placed a hand in the middle of his chest, trying to keep some distance between them. 'Why do you think Kouropoulos invited you here and then vanished?'

Zander shrugged, his eyes on her mouth. 'I really have no idea, and frankly I don't care. I'm enjoying the rest.'

'You haven't had much rest yet,' Lauranne teased and he gave her the sexiest smile she'd ever seen.

'Want to go back to bed?'

'No!' Her hunger for him appalled her, but she knew that it was all linked with the way she felt about him. And it was becoming harder and harder not to tell him.

* * *

They dined on their terrace, overlooking the pool and the beach, drinking wine and talking until darkness fell and the pool was lit by tiny lights spaced around the private garden.

The atmosphere was perfect and Zander was astonishingly good company, making her laugh with his dry observations about his business competitors and making her think and argue as he expressed his views on foreign affairs.

Enjoying herself hugely, Lauranne remembered just why she'd fallen so heavily under his spell five years earlier.

As well as being sophisticated, he was also well educated and astonishingly well informed about virtually everything. It was hardly surprising that her head had been turned.

And now, at last, she understood something of the life he'd had. The childhood that had made him the man he was now.

When they'd drunk the last of the wine and eaten the last of the food he took her hand and led her to the bedroom, stripping her clothes off with hands that were both gentle and urgent, his mouth seeking hers in the darkness.

After that, each day followed the same pattern.

They rose late, had breakfast by the pool and then explored the island by boat or on foot until it became too hot. Then they retreated to the villa and made love until Lauranne was exhausted.

By contrast, Zander never seemed tired. His stamina was awesome and on several occasions he chose to work on his laptop while Lauranne dozed on the huge bed. But the fact that he didn't leave her side, even when he was working, was intensely flattering.

It was almost as if he couldn't bear to be apart from her even for a moment, but that was ridiculous, of course. Zander was the most independent person she knew and he certainly didn't find her that irresistible.

It was probably the only place in the villa with a suitable plug, she thought practically, trying not to read anything into his behaviour.

'Don't you need sleep?' she asked him one day as she

lay wrapped in a sheet, so totally wiped out by the intensity of his lovemaking that she didn't think she'd ever be able to move again.

He flashed her a sizzling smile. 'Sex with you energises me, *agape mou*,' he confessed ruefully, leaning down to drop a lingering kiss on her mouth before picking up his laptop. 'And although I am here with you, unfortunately business does not stand still.'

'You're on holiday,' she said sleepily, struggling to keep her eyes from closing.

'It feels like a holiday,' he agreed, a frown touching his brows as if the thought had only just occurred to him, 'but it's supposed to be a business trip.'

The plump, perfect happiness oozed out of her.

Wrapped up in the fabulous atmosphere and his company, it actually felt more like a honeymoon, but he was right, of course. It *was* a business trip. And he'd brought her here for business reasons.

And on their fifth day, those business reasons were suddenly very much in evidence.

'That was Kouropoulos.' Zander tossed his phone onto the bed and reached for his shirt. 'He's back. He wants us to meet him and a member of his board for dinner tonight.'

'Oh.' So that was that, Lauranne thought bleakly.

'What's the matter?' Zander pulled the shirt on, his eyes narrowed as he looked at her. 'You look as though you just lost your best friend.'

'I've enjoyed it being just the two of us,' she said simply, her smile faltering at the sudden frown in his eyes.

Oh, help. Maybe she shouldn't have admitted that. Maybe—

'I've enjoyed it too,' Zander said gruffly, frowning as if the thought had only just occurred to him. 'But it isn't over yet. After dinner we'll be coming back here again so that I can ravish you.'

But despite his teasing words, he seemed different since

the call. For the past few days he'd relaxed. Seemed younger and more carefree. But now the international businessman was back.

And the honeymoon was over.

It was early evening when she glanced at her watch and realised that they should be getting ready. They were by the pool, Zander lying on a lounger next to her, engrossed in the business section of a paper, cool and relaxed.

She leaned over and dropped a kiss on his shoulder, closing her eyes as she breathed in his masculine scent. 'We should get dressed. We're expected for drinks on the terrace in half an hour.'

Zander tossed the newspaper to one side and sprang to his feet in an athletic movement, pulling her up after him. 'Wear something that covers everything. It's the only way I'll be able to keep my hands off you and I don't want to shock Kouropoulos.'

Lauranne gave a wistful smile. It was flattering that he wanted her so much, but a tiny part of her still desperately wished that it was more than just sex.

In the five days they'd been together they'd spent most of the time in bed, locked in the most passionate sex she'd ever experienced.

And when they were at their most intimate, she was finding it harder and harder not to tell him that she loved him.

Sooner or later the issue of a divorce was going to come up again, but she wasn't allowing herself to think about that now.

She was living for the present. Enjoying every minute while she could.

'You use the shower.' He took his mobile from his pocket and strolled towards the bedroom. 'I have some calls to make.'

Thinking that it would be nice if he weren't *quite* so easily distracted by work, Lauranne made her way to the bathroom and showered.

He was still on the phone, talking in Greek, when she walked into the bedroom ten minutes later wrapped in a huge fluffy bathrobe.

She selected underwear and a beautiful silk dress and let the bathrobe fall to the floor.

The flow of Greek immediately faltered and she glanced up to see Zander watching her hungrily, his attention very definitely *not* on his call.

Feeling wicked, she slid into her underwear and dress, pretending not to notice that he seemed to be having problems concentrating.

When he finally severed the connection, there was a faint sheen of sweat on his brow.

'In future don't undress in front of me when I'm on the phone,' he groaned, his eyes bright with amusement and something else that made her heart beat faster. 'I didn't actually hear a word my lawyer was saying.'

She tilted her head to one side and slipped her feet into her shoes, her expression innocent. 'You had trouble concentrating?'

'I haven't concentrated on anything much since I walked into your office three weeks ago,' he confessed ruefully and she felt a flash of satisfaction at the knowledge that she could affect him so strongly.

'So if I'm so distracting, why did you make me work for you?'

He flashed her a smile. 'Because you said no. I don't deal well with no.'

'So if I'd said yes you would have walked away?'

'There was never any chance of you saying yes,' he pointed out dryly. 'You have *never* said yes to me. It is a quirky part of your nature that you have to fight me.' He stared at her intently and then dragged his shirt over his head.

Her eyes were drawn to his broad chest, the tangle of dark hairs emphasising his intense masculinity.

The truth was she was fighting herself as much as him. Fighting the way she felt about him. He was the only man she'd ever met who had the ability to hurt her badly.

'So it was just about fighting me?' Something prompted her to ask the question and he sucked in a breath and looked at her through narrowed eyes, evidently considering her question seriously.

'No,' he said shortly, 'it wasn't about fighting you.'

Their eyes locked and her heart was suddenly pounding in her chest. 'Then what was it?'

He hesitated. 'You and I had unfinished business.'

'But if you'd known it was me, you never would have chosen my company.'

There was a brief pause. 'Yes, I would.'

Meaning what, exactly? Lauranne wondered, her eyes sliding over the powerful muscles of his chest.

'We are expected for drinks in fifteen minutes,' he drawled softly, 'and if you continue to look at me like that then we will be late. And I don't want to blow this deal.'

It was as if she'd dived head first into an arctic pool. Business always came first with Zander.

Even now, when sexual tension was throbbing in the air.

She gave him a cool smile and walked over to the mirror to apply her make-up. 'Of course you don't want to blow the deal.'

Without turning she unzipped her bag and selected a few cosmetics, pausing as she heard the sound of the shower.

Her fingers tightened around the tiny bottle she was holding. She could imagine him naked, the water sliding over every inch of his fabulously male body.

He was out in seconds, a towel slung round his hips as he rubbed his dark hair and reached for a small package from a drawer by the bed.

'I bought this for you.' He handed her a box almost casually but his eyes were intent on her face and her heart lurched crazily as fantasy overwhelmed her.

A small, prettily wrapped box.

Completely hypnotised by her own longing she stared at the box in his hand and he flipped it open.

She sucked in a breath, stunned by the beauty of the earrings nestling on the black velvet and by the depth of her own disappointment.

Had she really expected an engagement ring?

It was the one thing he'd never given her. Their marriage had been so quick that all she had was a gold band. A gold band that was currently lying in her drawer at home.

Was she really that deluded?

She looked up at him with a smile that revealed nothing of her thoughts. 'They're really beautiful, Zander.'

'Like you.'

She blushed at his softly spoken compliment and lifted the earrings from the box, placing them carefully in the palm of her hand. 'Why? Why did you buy me these?'

'To prove to you that I can be romantic,' Zander said lightly, lifting a hand and stroking her hair away from her face. 'Put them on. I know they'll suit you—'

She walked over to the mirror and slipped the earrings into her ears, noticing immediately that he was right. They did suit her.

'Thank you. I love—' she almost said *I love you* but stopped herself just in time '—them. I love them.'

His eyes met hers in the mirror and then he turned away and pulled on a fresh shirt and reached for his trousers.

Lauranne averted her eyes before the towel fell. Her insides were in enough of a state without being confronted with further evidence of his overwhelming virility.

She picked up her bag and moved to the door. 'I'll try not to let you down,' she said sweetly, her eyes challenging his, 'as long as you behave yourself.'

He laughed, slipped his mobile phone into his pocket and then gestured towards the door. 'I never behave myself where you're concerned. Now, are you ready?'

CHAPTER EIGHT

AS THEY took the steps to the terrace Zander tightened his grip on her hand,

'Remember, Anni, you are so in love with me that you can't see straight.'

Lauranne almost laughed at the irony. It was an almost perfect description of her true feelings.

But there was no way she was revealing that to him. In a way it would be refreshing to be able to show affection for him. Normally she kept her true feelings locked inside.

So it was a relief to smile adoringly at him as they strolled across the vine-covered terrace to meet Theo Kouropoulos.

A woman was standing by his side and as they drew closer Lauranne stopped dead, feeling the colour drain out of her face.

The happiness left her in a rush.

It was Marina, her ex-boss.

What was she doing here?

Lauranne stared at her in horror, a horror that deepened as she caught the venom in the older woman's expression.

'Welcome. I hope you enjoyed your day.' Kouropoulos stepped forward with a smile, shaking Zander's hand and greeting Lauranne warmly. 'My wife has stayed in Athens with my daughter, but may I introduce my Head of Corporate Affairs, Marina?'

Marina worked for Kouropoulos?

Lauranne had no choice but to take her outstretched hand, the effort of smiling so great that it made her cheeks ache.

'Lauranne and I know each other,' Marina said smoothly, her eyes so cold that Lauranne shivered.

'Marina worked for me in the past,' Zander confirmed, his

expression impossible to read as he surveyed the woman in front of him.

Lauranne looked at him in frustration. How could he behave so calmly?

'Then you should have taken better care of her.' Kouropoulos laughed and Lauranne ground her teeth.

Zander had taken extremely good care of Marina.

Ignoring Lauranne completely, Marina gave Zander a sultry smile and stepped closer, the slit in her dress parting to reveal an almost indecent length of thigh. 'Can I offer you a drink? Champagne?'

Lauranne watched in disbelief and misery as Zander took the proffered glass, smiling warmly at Marina, showing not one whit of discomfort.

She ground her teeth.

Did he have no conscience? He'd made love to her repeatedly since arriving on the island and now he was flirting openly with another woman. And not just any woman.

Marina was the woman he'd slept with five years before.

The woman who had destroyed their relationship.

Marina was the reason she'd sobbed in Tom's arms.

Showing no interest in the antics of his Corporate Affairs director, Theo Kouropoulos stepped up to her. 'So tell me, what do you think of our island?'

With considerable effort, Lauranne dragged her eyes away from Zander and Marina.

'It's beautiful,' she said honestly, glancing across the sand and battling with the temptation to drop her glass and make a run for it back to the privacy of the villa. 'Really beautiful.'

But inhabited by a snake.

Marina was still talking to Zander and the sight of their heads so close together, one so dark and one so fair, made sickness rise in her stomach.

How could he do this to her?

How could he so blatantly flaunt his ex-lover in front of her?

And from the way that Marina was looking at him she wasn't going to remain an ex for much longer.

Sickly, Lauranne considered another explanation. That the 'business' trip to the island had never been more than a ploy for him to spend time with Marina.

Was she just here to provide distraction?

To legitimise his relationship with his ex-lover?

'I hope you've been enjoying your time here,' Kouropoulos was saying. 'Zander and I will be getting down to work tomorrow, but Marina will be happy to entertain you.'

'I really wouldn't want to bother her,' Lauranne said quickly, so angry that she could barely speak. 'I'll have a lovely time just relaxing by the pool, I know I will.' Deciding to remind Marina just exactly who Zander was supposed to be with, she leaned towards him and lowered her eyelashes, her expression flirtatious. 'We've had a pretty exhausting few days, haven't we, darling?'

Not in the slightest bit discomforted by her blatant declaration of their relationship, Zander merely smiled and Kouropoulos joined in.

'This island is made for romance, Lauranne.'

Confused by Zander's lack of reaction, Lauranne fumed over the rest of her drink. Was he using her to make Marina jealous? Or was he using Marina to make *her* jealous? Deciding that whatever his game was, she wasn't playing it, she drained her drink and helped herself to another one, aware that Zander was watching her with a slight frown in his eyes.

Good, she thought crossly. If you think I'm going to play your little game, then you picked the wrong person.

She made small talk over drinks, ready to kill as she observed Zander and Marina locked in conversation the whole time.

'They have much to talk about,' Kouropoulos said gently,

topping up her glass again. 'Marina worked in his organisation, remember? What was your role in the company?'

'Mug,' Lauranne said clearly, her chin lifting as she fastened her blue gaze on Zander, who broke off his conversation and cast her a look of such ice-cold warning that she caught her breath.

Don't ruin this deal, his gaze said, and she flashed her eyes at him, the message clear.

Then don't mess with me.

If they'd had swords there would have been corpses lying on the terrace, but fortunately their only weapons were their eyes and they used them to the death.

'Lauranne was in a very junior position,' Zander said smoothly, his eyes still locked on her face as he telegraphed a clear warning. 'But she always showed potential.'

Marina frowned slightly at that, but Lauranne ignored her, reaching for her wine in the hope of numbing some of the fevered emotions surging around her body.

By the time they eventually sat down for dinner, her stomach was churning and anger was turning to misery.

How could she have been such a gullible fool?

Zander wasn't capable of committing to one woman, even when the sex was as exciting as it was between them.

Catching his narrowed glance, she remembered belatedly that she was supposed to look loving.

Well, tough, she thought miserably.

So far the only person who was looking loving was Marina, and she couldn't keep her hands off Zander.

Lauranne watched sickly, transported back five years.

She picked at her food, barely aware of the conversation around her until she heard Marina laugh.

'You men are *not* to discuss business at the dinner table,' she admonished gaily. 'Save it for tomorrow.'

Kouropoulos sipped his coffee and looked at Lauranne. 'Talking of business, you've done very well for yourself since you left Volakis Industries. I've seen some of the work you've done. Amazing.'

If Kouropoulos was aware of the extremely unsavoury details of her employment with Zander's company, then he was keeping it well hidden.

'Thank you.' Lauranne managed a polite smile. He seemed like a nice man. His only fault appeared to be his choice of employees.

'It's amazing how people grow and develop,' Marina said smoothly, the cold look in her eyes at odds with the fixed smile on her face. 'All those mistakes you made five years ago when you first worked for me must have paid off.'

Ignoring the sudden frown on Zander's face, Lauranne lifted her chin and looked Marina directly in the eye. 'The only mistake I made was falling in love with Zander.'

It was the first time she'd said those words out loud, but she knew that Zander wouldn't believe her anyway. He'd think that she was just acting her part.

Kouropoulos gave her a searching look. 'If you were so in love, how come your marriage lasted such a short time?'

The directness of his question threw her and she couldn't prevent her eyes sliding back to Marina.

In the end it was Zander who answered. 'We had some differences,' he said smoothly, reaching for his wineglass and lifting it towards her in a silent toast, 'but we've resolved them.'

Lauranne sat silent, finding it harder and harder to play the game he wanted her to play. Anger rising inside her, she gave up the pretence of eating and lowered her fork to her plate.

'Zander wasn't ready to commit to anyone then.' She looked at Zander but his expression was veiled by thick dark lashes as he lounged in his chair, watching her. She shifted her gaze to Marina, a spark of challenge in her eyes. 'He was still enjoying the concept of variety.'

She saw Marina's colour deepen in anger and braced herself for confrontation, reminding herself firmly that she wasn't an employee any more. This woman couldn't do *any-thing* to her.

But even so her palms were damp and her heart was beating so rapidly that she felt faint.

'Zander has always played the field,' Kouropoulos said dryly, 'but let's hope that now that you're back together again, that will all end.'

Hardly, Lauranne thought to herself, with Marina within such easy reach.

'So how did you two rediscover each other?' Kouropoulos didn't so much as glance in Marina's direction but Zander did and his expression was suddenly thoughtful.

'Lauranne and I have been in touch for some months,' he drawled casually, 'but we only came together properly a few weeks ago.'

'That's very romantic.'

'And quite a lengthy relationship for Zander,' Marina interjected cattily. 'It's almost time you moved on again, don't you think?'

Something gleamed in his eyes and he reached across the table to take Lauranne's hands in his. 'I won't be moving on.'

As an actor he was thoroughly convincing, Lauranne brooded, resisting the temptation to snatch her hand away and slap him hard.

There'd be time for that later when they were in private.

In the meantime she didn't want to give Marina the satisfaction of knowing that she'd succeeded in stimulating tension between them.

So she just stared at him, hurt and accusation brimming in her blue eyes. It was no good him pretending to be her lover, she thought, when his real lover was seated next to him.

Suddenly she couldn't stand it any longer. Couldn't stand the pretence. Where in their deal had it said that he was allowed to flaunt other relationships? She rose to her feet and cast an apologetic glance towards Theo Kouropoulos. 'I'm so sorry to be rude, but I'm really tired. Would you mind if I had an early night?'

'Of course not. You do look a little pale.' He rose to his feet too and gestured to Zander. 'You must go with her. We'll see you tomorrow at ten.'

'Why don't you drop her back at the villa and then join us for another drink on the terrace?' Marina said smoothly, stepping round the table and placing a possessive hand on Zander's arm. 'It's *far* too early to be going to bed.'

'Well, that depends…' Kouropoulos laughed, exchanging looks of male understanding with Zander. 'My guess is that we won't be seeing these two until tomorrow's meeting.'

Marina's mouth tightened angrily but then she relaxed and forced a smile. 'In that case I'll see you at the meeting too. Theo has asked me to join in the negotiations.'

Lauranne glanced at Zander to gauge his reaction but as usual his face was expressionless.

They exchanged goodnights and Lauranne took the path that led back to their villa, Zander close by her side.

Careful not to let even one part of her body brush against him, she stalked down the prettily lit path, her high heels tapping rhythmically as she tried to walk off her anger.

The moment they stepped inside the villa she slammed the door shut and let all the pain and the humiliation pour forth.

'How *dare* you? How dare you bring me here knowing that that woman, your—your—how *could* you?' She broke off with a choked sob, *hating* herself for being so out of control but too utterly miserable to be anything else.

Zander stood frozen to the spot, clearly stunned by her attack. 'I have absolutely no idea what you're talking about,' he said coldly. 'But I do know that if you carry on behaving the way you behaved tonight then you're going to blow the deal.'

'I don't care about your stupid, rotten deal,' she lied, tears spilling onto her cheeks. 'I only care that you brought me here knowing that *that* woman would be here too—'

Zander swore fluently in Greek and sucked in a breath. 'Firstly I did *not* know that Marina was going to be here, and secondly I don't understand your problem. I can understand that it may feel a little awkward that you once worked for her, but it was a long time ago—'

'And that's supposed to make it OK?' She was so angry that her whole body was shaking. 'Well, let me tell you something, Zander, there is *never* a good time to introduce *your wife* to your mistress! And awkward is certainly not the word I'd choose to use to describe this situation.'

There was a pulsing silence, broken only by the fractured sound of her breathing.

Underneath his tan, Zander lost his colour and his eyes glittered dangerously. 'Mistress? You're suggesting that Marina is my *mistress?*'

'I don't know.' She spread her hands, her eyes flashing with anger. 'You tell me, Zander. I know she *used* to be. As for whether it's still going on—what exactly *is* this deal you're negotiating with Kouropoulos? Does it include his director of Corporate Affairs?'

'That's enough.' With a growl of anger he stepped forward and closed his hands around the tops of her arms. 'You're not making any sense. I assumed you were upset because Marina was your boss and she was there when I fired you. I assumed that was the reason why you were so quiet over dinner—because you were embarrassed—'

She lifted her chin, her eyes blazing with passion and pride. 'I have *nothing* to be embarrassed about. I did nothing wrong. You were the one who was wrong to fire me! But that should be on your conscience, not mine.'

He closed his eyes briefly and muttered under his breath. 'Which accusation am I dealing with here? Let's go back to the mistress. Why are you suggesting that Marina is my mistress?'

'Because she used to be and tonight you seemed extremely

pleased to see her,' Lauranne said bitterly, trying to pull away from him.

His grip tightened on her arms, holding her firm. 'Listen to me carefully, Lauranne, because I'm not in the habit of repeating myself.' His voice was dangerously soft. 'I have *never* had an affair with Marina.'

'How can you say that?' She looked at him, pain shimmering in her eyes. 'She was in your office. Naked.'

He looked at her with a convincing lack of comprehension. *'When?'* He gave her a shake, his dark eyes suddenly blazing with an emotion that she didn't recognise. 'When was she *ever* naked in my office?'

'That night you found me with Tom! What did you think I'd do, Zander?' She struggled in his arms but he still held her fast, refusing to let her go, his strong fingers biting into her soft flesh. 'Behave like a good little wife and wait quietly for you to come back to me?'

She twisted violently and this time he let her go, his handsome face blank of expression as his hands fell to his sides.

'I want you to tell me exactly what happened that night,' he said harshly, his breathing rapid. 'And don't miss out anything.'

She closed her eyes and choked back a sob. 'It was bad enough the first time. Do I really have to relive it?'

'Every detail.' His jaw was set aggressively and she took a deep breath.

'He wants to see me?' Lauranne put down the list of journalists that she'd been amending, unable to suppress the smile. 'Right now?'

'It seems your husband can't get enough of you.' Tom, her colleague, observed, a trace of sarcasm in his tone as he relayed the message.

Lauranne got to her feet. 'I thought he was working.'

'I don't think his mind is on his work,' Tom said shortly. 'And it hasn't been for the past two months. You've done what no one else has managed. You've finally snared the boss.'

Lauranne frowned at his tone. She'd really enjoyed working with Tom, but he'd changed towards her since her relationship with Zander had begun. Snared the boss. 'You make it sound awful.'

It sounded so cool and calculating and that wasn't what had happened at all. She'd fallen in love. And even if Zander had never actually said those words to her yet, he would one day. And in the meantime—well, he'd married her, hadn't he? For a man like Zander, a man with a reputation for avoiding commitment, his gesture meant more than words, surely?

'Better get yourself up there,' Tom said lightly. 'You don't want to keep the man waiting.'

Unable to contain the bubble of happiness, Lauranne nodded. 'OK. If anyone wants to know where I am, I'll—'

'Lauranne, you're with the boss.' Tom's voice had an edge to it. 'Who's going to question it? And anyway, I'm off to the bar for a drink.'

Lauranne bit her lip, reflecting that Tom clearly had some sort of problem with her relationship. And he seemed to be drinking more and more. 'Right.'

Too excited at the prospect of seeing Zander in the middle of the working day, she pushed the thought away, resolving to have a frank discussion with Tom later. They'd been firm friends since the day she'd started working at Volakis Industries. They'd be able to sort out any problems.

Her heart thudding with anticipation, she straightened her scarlet silk skirt and on impulse released her hair from its pony-tail. It fell softly onto her shoulders and she swung her head a few times, knowing that this was the way Zander loved it.

Only one more week and they'd be leaving the Caribbean hotel where they'd met and married and returning to his home in Athens.

She took the path that led to his suite of offices, thrilled that he couldn't make it through a working day without seeking her out.

He might not have said he loved her, but he was showing all the signs.

She pushed open the door, expecting to see one of the secretaries, but the reception area was empty, a half-drunk cup of coffee abandoned by the computer.

Wondering why the place was so empty, Lauranne made straight for his office, tapping lightly on the door and pushing it open.

For a moment she thought this room was empty too. And then she saw her.

Wearing only a bathrobe, her blonde hair tousled, her lipstick smeared across her mouth.

'Marina?' Lauranne choked the word out and her boss clutched the bathrobe.

'Lauranne.' Her gaze flickered guiltily towards another door that Lauranne knew led to a bathroom. She heard the sound of a shower running and then Zander's deep voice, instructing Marina to leave the papers on the desk.

Feeling physically sick, Lauranne stared at her boss in disgust and disbelief. 'How *could* you?'

'You didn't really think he was exclusive to you, did you?' Marina's eyes flashed bright with triumph. 'When I wanted him, he came right back to me.'

The noise from the shower stopped and Lauranne knew that any moment now Zander would be coming back into the room and she'd have to face him.

Her emotions and her faith shattered into tiny pieces, she backed out of the office and then turned and ran down the path, her blonde hair flying across her face as she fled from betrayal.

'Lauranne?' Tom's voice penetrated her shocked brain and she stopped dead, looking at him blankly.

'Lauranne!' Tom's voice was urgent. 'What's wrong?'

She was shaking so badly she could barely stand and Tom

slipped an arm around her shoulders. 'You'd better come back to my room—it's closest.'

Without questioning his intentions she followed him like someone in a trance and only when the door closed behind her did she start to cry.

And then she couldn't stop.

She sobbed on Tom's chest, clutching at his shirt as she tried to tell him what had happened, incoherent with grief.

For a moment he stood there, rigid, and then he gave a groan and the next minute she was on the bed with him and he was muttering drunkenly into her neck.

'Forget him, Lauranne. He's not worth it.'

'Tom?' Totally shocked for the second time in one evening, Lauranne tried to wriggle from underneath him but he slid his body over hers, pinning her to the bed.

'You're *so* beautiful. I've always wanted you—you must know that.'

No, she didn't know that. Horrified by his announcement, Lauranne surfaced from the depths of misery.

'Tom, for goodness' sake!' She pushed at his chest and wriggled under him but before she could free herself she heard the door to the room open and she looked up to see Zander standing there, his eyes black with anger.

Flayed raw by his betrayal, she froze and thought, *you bastard,* and then turned her mouth to Tom's.

Zander watched her in silence, his whole body vibrating with tension.

'Who told you that I wanted to see you that night?'

Lauranne shook her head. 'I don't know— Tom took the call—'

Zander's hard mouth tightened. 'I want you to tell me exactly what I said when I was in the shower.'

'I—I don't know—'

'Well, think!' His tone was thickened and pulsing with urgency. 'I want you to remember what I said. It's important.'

She looked at him with a total lack of comprehension. How could it possibly be important? What did it matter what he'd said? He'd slept with the woman. 'I—I think you were saying something about a guest list.' She frowned and then nodded. 'Yes, you told her to leave the guest list on the table.'

His jaw tensed. 'And then what happened?'

'The shower stopped and I looked at her—' Her voice cracked and she cleared her throat. 'She—she—'

'She what?' His voice was rough and Lauranne took a step backwards.

'She smiled. She obviously wanted me to catch the two of you together.'

'But we weren't together, were we, Lauranne?' he said savagely, taking a step towards her, his eyes fixed on her pale face. 'I was in the shower and she was in my office.'

'She was naked!'

'Was she?'

She stared at him, heart pounding. 'You know she was—'

'No, I don't,' he said, speaking deliberately so that there could be no misunderstanding. 'I remember her coming to my office that evening and I remember being intensely irritated and concerned that she was becoming so overt in her attempts to seduce me. I made quite sure that I didn't leave the shower until my office was empty. I certainly didn't know that you were there.'

Lauranne froze, her brain suddenly confused as she ran through the events of that night a further time, this time applying a different interpretation. Was he seriously suggesting that nothing had happened?

'*Attempts* to seduce you?'

Was he really trying to tell her that they'd never had an affair?

'Let me fill in the rest of the evening,' he said, his mouth set in a grim line. 'By the time I left the shower my office was empty—presumably both you and Marina had flown by then. Almost immediately I received a call from Marina saying that she'd seen you with Tom and that you were very upset. Naturally I came to find you.'

Naturally?

'Y-you cared that I was upset?' She stared at him blankly and he gave a humourless laugh.

'We were married. Of course I cared. Foolishly, as it turned out. I found you kissing Farrer.'

Lauranne shook her head. 'I don't know what came over him that night. He'd been drinking—he wasn't himself. He'd been behaving oddly all day. And then he jumped on me. When you walked through the door I was hurt and angry and I wanted to show you that I didn't care.'

There was a long silence and Zander stared at her, his eyes glittering. 'Finally I'm beginning to understand what happened. You kissed Farrer to make me jealous because you thought I'd just betrayed you with Marina. Do you know the risk you took?' he asked hoarsely. 'I could have *killed* him for being with you—'

She flinched slightly, remembering that moment all too well. 'You gave him a black eye and a nosebleed and I wasn't *with* him.'

'But you made damn sure that I thought that you were.' He stared at her for a long moment and then turned and paced the length of the villa, tension visible in every line of his powerful frame. 'If we weren't both so stubborn and hotheaded things might not have exploded so badly.'

'We were manipulated, Zander,' she said simply. 'Both of us. And then you fired me. On the spot. ''Get out,'' you said, ''I never want to see you again.'' '

He sucked in a breath, a muscle working in his lean jaw. 'I'm willing to admit that on that occasion my judgement may have been flawed—'

'It wasn't flawed, Zander,' she muttered. 'It was totally distorted.'

His eyes flashed defensively. 'I had just found you in bed with another man— I was *jealous*.'

'And so was I.'

Breathing heavily, he gave a twisted smile. 'But neither of us had reason, it would seem. It would help our relationship a great deal if we talked instead of fighting. Why didn't you ask me about Marina? Why didn't you shout at me then? Why didn't you black my eye? If I'd known what you were thinking then I could have put you right immediately—'

'Because I had no reason to doubt what I saw,' she shot back. 'She was naked and you were in the shower.'

'I left the robe in my office,' Zander recalled, a frown touching his dark brows. 'She must have pulled it on over her clothes to make you think she was naked.'

Lauranne stared at him. 'Over her clothes?'

He shrugged. 'Who knows? And it really doesn't matter anyway. Why did you have so little faith in me?'

She swallowed hard. 'Because I suppose deep down I couldn't believe my luck,' she mumbled. 'Everyone wanted you, Zander. You're an international heartthrob. I'd been expecting it to happen at some point. It just came earlier than even I'd expected—'

Dark eyes crashed into hers. 'Meaning what, exactly?'

'You don't do commitment and you never did,' she said, her eyes sliding away from his. 'Women chase you endlessly. The temptation is always there. I was always afraid that sooner or later you'd find someone else.'

Waiting, aching, hoping it wouldn't happen—

He looked at her, his eyes glittering strangely. 'And you married me, believing that?'

She dragged her eyes away from his, afraid of giving too much away. 'We were both impulsive—'

'So you assumed the worst of me—'

Her eyes shot back to his in defiance. 'As you did of me.'

They glared at each other and then he gave a long sigh and raked long fingers through his cropped hair, a rueful expression on his handsome face.

'The problem is that we are both equally stubborn,' he said

dryly. 'You were determined not to let me know that I'd hurt you and I was too jealous and angry to look deeper.'

Lauranne licked her lips. 'You really weren't having an affair with her?'

'This is the first time in my life I've ever repeated myself,' he gritted, walking towards her and taking her hands in his. 'But no, I wasn't.'

She closed her eyes. 'Oh, God—'

What had they both done?

He slid his hands into her hair and tilted her face to his, forcing her to look at him.

'She was trying to break up our relationship.'

Lauranne nodded sickly. 'I already reached that conclusion myself.'

'She thought she was in love with me,' he said, his tone matter-of-fact, his thumbs gently massaging her cheeks as he stared down into her eyes. 'Your arrival on the scene must have been very hard for her to cope with. You were young, clever, stunningly beautiful and I was totally captivated. It must have been obvious to everyone that I was seriously smitten with you.'

Totally captivated? Seriously smitten? Reminding herself that he was still just talking about sex, she looked at him blankly.

'How would it have been obvious?'

Until their whirlwind marriage, most of their relationship had been conducted behind closed doors or on boats or quiet corners of deserted beaches. She certainly wasn't aware that they'd had an audience.

'I didn't do a stroke of work for the entire two months we were together,' he confessed in that lazy drawl that always made her knees shake. 'My staff were in a state of shock.'

They were?

'So you think Marina—'

'I think she got rid of you in the only way possible.' His

expression was thoughtful. 'She knew that I was Greek enough to be blinded by jealousy.'

'But she couldn't have known I'd turn to Tom.'

Zander looked at her and his jaw tightened. 'You and he were pretty close.'

Lauranne bit her lip. 'I was wrong too—stubborn.' Her heart beating faster, she stood on tiptoe and pressed her mouth against his.

With a tortured groan he returned the kiss, his tongue sliding into her mouth, seeking more intimate contact.

'We *both* need to use our minds more than our feelings,' he said ruefully, lifting her in his arms and carrying her through to the bedroom.

'What are you doing?' Her arms tightened around his neck and he shot her a smile that was pure, conquering male.

'I'm not risking any more bruising on that marble. We both need comfort.'

This time when he stripped her naked his hands were gentle, his mouth and fingers torturing them both as he drove them to fever pitch before making love to her so slowly that when her climax hit she wrapped her arms around his broad shoulders and sobbed with emotion.

'Don't cry.' He brushed her tears away with long fingers, his breathing still rapid as he rolled onto his back, taking her with him. 'I *never* want to see you cry.'

She had to bite her lip to prevent herself from declaring her love for him.

Instead she buried her face in his warm flesh, loving the feel of him against her burning cheek.

'So what happens now?' After a moment she lifted her head to look at him. 'Marina will ruin this deal for you if she can.'

'That won't happen.'

'She's devious.'

He turned to look at her, his dark eyes intent as they searched hers. 'I know what she is, *agape mou*. And you have no reason at all to be jealous. After all, you are the one in my bed.'

The one in his bed.

She held him tight, feeling the warmth of his skin and his solid strength, wondering what it would take to be in his heart, too. 'What if he doesn't sell to you?'

'He'll sell.' He dropped a kiss on her mouth. 'Now get some sleep.'

Zander walked out onto the terrace, glancing back at the bed where Lauranne slept soundly. Unfortunately he'd never been further from sleep in his life. Their conversation kept replaying in his head and he found himself suffering from an emotion that was entirely new to him.

Guilt.

She'd been just twenty-one and at the beginning of her career and yet he'd crushed her ruthlessly.

A lesser person would have been destroyed by his actions. But not Lauranne.

He gave a humourless laugh as he stared across the dimly lit swimming pool that adjoined their private villa.

Why had he done that?

Never, before or since, had he treated a person quite so mercilessly as he'd treated Lauranne.

The guilt grew in intensity, weighing down his mind and his body.

He shifted slightly but the feeling stayed with him, lodged inside him, a constant reminder of his crime.

He'd never once listened to an explanation from her.

He'd just assumed she was like all the other women he'd met in his life, unfaithful and money-grabbing.

He'd wanted her out of his company and out of his life as fast as possible.

And it was only now that he was asking himself why.

He glanced backwards to the woman lying asleep on the bed, his gaze resting on her golden hair, spread in soft waves across both pillows, and suddenly he knew the reason why. He'd needed to get rid of her because she'd been a threat to his emotional well-being.

For the first time in his life he'd cared about a woman.

For the first time in his life he'd given a woman the power to hurt him. The same way that his mother had hurt his father.

For the first time in his life, he'd been in love.

Zander closed his eyes, accepting the truth.

Love was the reason he'd married her. That elusive reason that he'd never been able to identify. And love was the reason that he'd never sought a divorce.

It had been love that had fuelled his unreasonable jealousy that night he'd found her with Farrer. And it had been self-protection that had driven him to fire her without even giving her a fair hearing.

It was no wonder she'd fought him when he'd ordered her to work for him again. Her last experience of working for him must have left her so traumatised that she could hardly be blamed for not wishing to repeat the experience.

And he'd bullied her into doing it anyway, using the gratitude and love she felt for Farrer as a tool to get his own way.

Facing the fact that there was no way she would have chosen to be here if he hadn't forced the issue, he gritted his teeth and acknowledged that he was about to face the biggest challenge of his life. Persuading her that a divorce was *not* a good idea.

They had breakfast on the terrace, overlooking the private swimming pool.

It was utterly peaceful, the vines providing shade from the warmth of the sun.

Zander seemed unusually tense but, after a few questioning looks in his direction, Lauranne decided that it must be the strain of the forthcoming meeting. She knew just how badly he wanted the island.

She nibbled a roll and looked at him, her cheeks heating as she remembered just how affectionate he'd been the night before. But that didn't mean anything, she reminded herself hastily. Zander was a skilled lover and he knew exactly how to make a woman feel good.

He was still looking at her, inscrutable as ever. 'Why are you still working with Tom?'

Surprised by the question, she gave a little shrug. 'We built the business together.' She looked at him warily, reluctant to even mention Tom's name in his presence. 'It's never occurred to me to leave. Obviously I didn't have any money, so he provided all the finance—'

'Ah, yes—money.' Zander leaned back in his chair. 'Why did you marry me, Lauranne?'

The question came out of nowhere and she looked at him in appalled silence, wondering whether her feelings had shown on her face. Had he guessed just how much she loved him?

Summoning up a casual smile, she shrugged, refusing to reveal her own vulnerability in the face of his cool detachment.

'As you said, great sex and a credit card without a limit. What more could a girl want?'

His eyes narrowed. 'What more, indeed?' He paused, his expression thoughtful, and when he spoke again his voice was soft. 'Except you never actually used my credit card, did you? You never spent a single penny of my money, Lauranne.'

'I didn't have time,' she said lightly and he gave a wry smile.

'Most of the women I know could work their way through a small fortune in less time that it takes to put up your hair.'

'I'm not most women.'

'You think you need to tell me that?' He gave her a speculative look and she shifted uncomfortably, wondering where this conversation was leading.

'Look, we both know the marriage was a mistake and obviously when this is all over we'll—'

'Why was it a mistake?'

His casual question threw her in mid-sentence and she broke off and gaped at him. Why was it a mistake?

Because he hadn't loved her.

She stuffed her hands in her shorts and wondered how they ever managed to last five minutes without killing each other. 'What we shared was sex, Zander. Not a great basis for marriage.'

She swallowed, forced to acknowledge again the gulf between their emotions. For her their relationship had been everything, a fierce, tempestuous rightness that she knew she'd never find with another man. For him it had been great sex.

He was looking at her, a strange expression in his eyes. 'It's not just sex. You excite me more than any woman I've ever met but I also get a kick out of the rest of our relationship. You're sparky and sharp and interesting to be around.'

'You mean I'm the only person who isn't afraid to say no to you.'

He laughed, genuinely amused. 'Plenty of people say no to me, Anni. I'm not quite the tyrant you believe me to be.'

She caught her breath, transfixed by the charm of his smile and the light in his eyes. 'I don't think you're a tyrant.'

She remembered the people she'd interviewed in his company, all of whom had spoken of Zander with a respect bordering on the reverential.

Their eyes locked and he gave a low groan. 'Don't look at me like that. I have to meet Kouropoulos in less than half an hour.' He rose to his feet and held out a hand. 'I want you to come with me.'

She stared at him. 'You do?'

'Absolutely.'

She swallowed. 'But Marina—'

'Surely you're not afraid of Marina,' he said softly, his eyes challenging her. 'You flash sparks and anger for me whenever I put one foot out of line. What's stopping you doing the same with her?'

She hesitated. 'Because she's evil. And clever. I can't prove what she did. It's all circumstantial.'

He shrugged. 'So we make her confess.'

She gave a laugh. 'Thumbscrews and torture chambers, Zander?'

'Now there's a thought.' His eyes gleamed wickedly and she blushed.

'Don't.' She felt the heat rise inside her under his steady gaze. How could it be possible to want a man this much? 'It isn't a joke. She wants you, Zander.'

His eyes narrowed, his gaze blatantly sexual. 'But I'm taken.'

Of course. The sudden reminder of exactly why she was here struck Lauranne like a physical blow.

Her role was to convince Kouropoulos that she and Zander were in love.

None of it was real.

But then she remembered his promise to his grandmother and she lifted her chin and smiled. 'Then let's go to this meeting and remind them both of that.'

CHAPTER NINE

THEO Kouropoulos scanned through the papers in front of him.

Lauranne stared at the table, terrified that her face might reveal something it shouldn't. She wasn't used to playing these elaborate business games. Zander wanted the island. She *knew* he wanted the island, but his body language said that he was totally indifferent to the outcome of the meeting.

He sprawled in a chair on the other side of the table looking thoroughly relaxed and slightly bored.

He was the master of negotiation, outsmarting his opponent at every turn.

Finally Kouropoulos lifted his head, his expression hard. 'You're planning to close the resort.'

Zander didn't flinch. 'That's right.'

There was a heavy silence and Kouropoulos shifted in his chair, his voice gruff as he spoke. 'I've been here for twenty-six years.'

'I know exactly how long you've had possession of this island.' Thick dark lashes shielded his eyes but there was a tension in his powerful frame that hadn't been there before.

'The business is losing money,' Kouropoulos admitted ruefully, 'but with an injection of capital—'

'I'm not interested in saving the resort,' Zander said shortly, his tone totally lacking in emotion. 'I want the island for an entirely different reason.'

Kouropoulos sat back in his chair, one eyebrow raised. 'And that reason is—?'

Zander smiled. *'Personal.'*

Lauranne glanced at him, knowing exactly what the reason was and loving him all the more for it.

Theo Kouropoulos was looking at Zander thoughtfully. He opened his mouth and began to speak in English, and then he glanced briefly at Marina and Lauranne and switched to rapid Greek, making sure that the only person who could understand him was Zander.

Zander sat still, his eyes fixed on the older man.

When Kouropoulos finally finished speaking, Zander replied in the same tongue, nothing in his expression giving even the slightest clue as to the content of the discussion.

Lauranne wished she'd bothered to learn Greek.

She had absolutely no idea what was being said, and neither had Marina if the look of frustration on her over-made-up face was anything to go by, but she could tell by the body language of the two men that it was significant.

Suddenly she realised that Kouropoulos was looking at her with a beaming smile on his face.

Uncomprehending, she glanced at Zander for some clue as to how she should respond and he smiled at her.

'I was just revealing our plans, *agape mou.*'

Plans?

Lauranne managed a suitably vague smile and Kouropoulos chuckled.

'You are going to break the hearts of millions of women, Lauranne. And I have to admit that I was beginning to give up hope that Zander would ever mend his marriage.'

Mend his marriage?

Just what exactly had Zander said?

Her breathing in a mess, Lauranne looked at Zander for inspiration or explanation, afraid to say the wrong thing.

'I've told him that we won't be getting a divorce,' Zander said softly, his gaze fixing on her shocked face. 'Ever. I've told him that I want the island as a home for my wife and children.'

She stared into his eyes, only dimly aware of Marina's shocked denial.

For one short, amazing moment she allowed herself the luxury of believing he meant it.

And then she remembered how badly he wanted the island.

Of course he didn't mean it.

Kouropoulos gave a delighted laugh. 'I never thought I'd see the day—'

'Neither did I,' Zander drawled, his eyes still holding Lauranne's, 'but that was before I fell in love.'

Marina sucked in a breath. 'So if you're staying married, why isn't she wearing a ring?'

Zander smiled. 'Her wedding ring is being adjusted.' Dragging his gaze away from Lauranne, his eyes hardened as he looked at Marina. 'And next time it won't be leaving her finger.'

His expression was cold and his tone held a blatant warning. Marina's face lost its colour as she understood the message he was conveying.

Kouropoulos chuckled, seemingly oblivious to the undercurrent of tension in the room. 'The female population will weep buckets.'

Starting with Marina, Lauranne thought cynically, noting that the other woman's eyes had hardened, her face a mask of anger.

As if by telepathy, Marina lifted her gaze and stared at Lauranne in blatant challenge. 'Zander will do and say anything to get what he wants,' she said smoothly and Kouropoulos frowned at her.

'Marina—'

She shot him a look of contempt. 'Surely you don't believe him, Theo? This whole reconciliation is staged for your benefit! His marriage was a sham! It lasted a month and it's hardly surprising when you look at his track record. Zander Volakis will never settle down with one woman. But he'd say anything to get his hands on this island.'

Lauranne caught her breath. It was true, of course, but if

Marina could persuade Kouropoulos that she was right then Zander had lost the island.

The island that meant so much to him.

'It isn't staged.' She spoke clearly, her smile faltering as she looked first at Kouropoulos and then at Zander. 'And I suppose that makes me the luckiest woman in the world.'

Brilliant dark eyes flared with masculine triumph as they meshed with hers and Marina let out a breath in a hiss.

'For goodness' sake, Theo. Stop playing the romantic and look at the facts. They've been separated for five years. He fired her!'

'Our relationship has always been tempestuous,' Zander agreed huskily, reaching out a hand and taking Lauranne's in his, the warmth and strength of his fingers stoking the dying embers of her courage. 'And that is part of the attraction for both of us. But in fighting, we have wasted much time. Too much time.'

He lifted her hand to his lips and she felt her heart twist.

He was *so* convincing.

Marina glared at Lauranne. 'Once he has the island, he won't need you any more.'

'I will always need Lauranne,' Zander drawled, a strange look in his eyes as he looked at her. Then he turned his attention back to Kouropoulos. 'So will you sell?'

The older man nodded. 'Yes. It is exactly as your father would have wished.'

Zander tensed slightly but didn't respond, rising to his feet in a fluid movement. 'My lawyer will be here in a few hours. He can sort out the details with your people.'

Kouropoulos nodded, standing up and reaching out a hand. 'I hope you'll stay with us for a few more days.'

'Yes, do stay.' Suddenly back to her professional self, Marina smiled at both of them. 'It's a shame to rush off when things are just getting—interesting.'

Lauranne felt herself stiffen. She didn't trust the woman an inch. Why would she want them to stay?

As they left the main house Lauranne glanced at Zander anxiously. 'She's very upset.'

He shrugged, supremely indifferent. 'She'll get over it.'

Lauranne bit her lip, feeling anything but reassured.

Past experience had taught her just how destructive Marina could be when jealous. And surely at the moment she must be feeling very jealous indeed?

Later that afternoon, Zander went back to the main house to finalise some of the details with Kouropoulos and Lauranne took advantage of the time on her own to have a swim in the private pool attached to the villa.

She slid into the pool, enjoying the feel of the cool water against her heated skin.

Feeling surprisingly relaxed, she swam length after length and then floated on her back with her eyes closed.

'Don't tell me.' A familiar voice came from the doorway of the villa. 'He's dumped you again so you're trying to drown yourself.'

Her eyes flew open and she gasped in surprise and delight. 'Tom! What are you doing here?'

He walked to the edge of the pool, a wry smile playing around his mouth. 'Rescuing you from your folly?'

Deciding that the middle of a swimming pool wasn't the place to conduct a conversation, Lauranne swam quickly to the side and pulled herself out, reaching for the nearest towel.

She wrapped herself up and then padded across to give Tom a hug. 'So I ask you again, what are you doing here?'

She hadn't even told him where she was going. Just that she was going to take a week off. How had he found her?

'Yes, do answer that question, Farrer.' Zander's voice, hard and simmering with all-male fury, came from the doorway behind them and Lauranne pulled away quickly, feeling horribly guilty even though she'd done nothing wrong.

Zander prowled onto the terrace with lethal menace, his gaze fixed firmly on Tom, who'd gone incredibly pale.

'I was worried. Lauranne dashed off without any explanation,' he said stiffly, 'and I wanted to see her. To check that she's all right.'

'And now you've seen her,' Zander said silkily, 'you can leave.'

Lauranne saw the raw anger in his dark eyes and held her breath, horror holding her fixed to the spot. It was like a replay of five years previously. And then she saw Marina in the background, her face alight with satisfaction as she stood next to her astonished boss.

Marina—

Anger shot through Lauranne and suddenly she knew exactly why Tom had suddenly arrived on the island. She turned to Tom, an urgent look on her face. 'You didn't need to come. I'm fine. I'd like you to go, Tom. I'm honestly OK.'

Dear God, how could Marina have done this?

Tom's presence was the one thing guaranteed to goad Zander into an unthinking fury.

And that had been her intention, of course—

Tom wasn't looking at her. His eyes were fixed on Zander. 'I'm not leaving without you, Lauranne. I know you're only here to help him clinch his precious deal and if you ask me you've done enough for the guy—'

Lauranne looked at him in confusion. 'Tom, *please*—'

Tom was glaring at Zander. 'I *won't* let you hurt her again. She loves you so much she'd do anything for you. When you're around she does utterly crazy things and I won't let you take advantage of that.'

Lauranne gave a tiny moan. 'Tom—'

He ignored her plea. 'You broke her into a million tiny pieces,' he said hoarsely, his hands curling into fists by his sides. 'Every morning I used to have to drag her out of bed and force her to go to work, when all she wanted to do was curl up and die. And you did that to her, Volakis. You threw her out and you didn't *once* check that she was OK. You left that to me. I was the one who had to put her together again.'

Zander sucked in a breath, his dark eyes glittering. 'I'm well aware of that.'

Tom shook his head. 'Well, you're not doing it to her again,' he growled, taking a step forward, his fists clenched by his sides. 'She may love you too much to say no to you, but I won't let you take advantage of her. If you want the island then you do it without this pretence of getting back together.'

Kouropoulos stepped forward, a disapproving frown on his face as he looked at Zander.

'So Marina was right. This *reconciliation* was all a set-up to persuade me that I should sell the island.' He shook his head in distaste. 'The deal is off, Volakis.'

Zander didn't even look at him.

Instead his eyes were fixed on Tom. And then his gaze shifted to Lauranne, a funny smile that she couldn't interpret touching his firm mouth. There was a strange light in his eyes and his breathing wasn't quite steady. And then, without uttering a word, he turned and strode away from the villa without a backward glance.

Lauranne watched him go and anxiety ripped through her. Did he still think that there was something going on between her and Tom?

For a frantic moment was tempted to run after him, but she stopped herself in time. What was the point? Zander didn't want her. He'd proved that by walking away. All he'd wanted was the island, and thanks to Marina he'd lost it.

'Oh, dear, what a shame,' Marina cooed smugly and Lauranne whirled on her, all thoughts of discretion forgotten as her anger rose to the surface with frightening speed.

'How dare you? Do you know what you've done?' Her voice shook as she stepped towards the other woman, totally ignoring the others, who were watching her passionate outburst in astonishment. *'Do you know what you've done?'*

Marina lifted her chin but she took a step backwards, her expression suddenly alarmed. *'I* haven't done anything,' she said, her face a picture of innocence. 'You and Zander have done it all with your deceit and your lies.'

Lauranne shook her head, so angry and worried about Zander that she could barely speak. 'There was no deceit. I love Zander and I always have. The only reason our relationship crashed five years ago is because *you* worked so hard to make it happen and *you're* the reason it's crashing again now.' Her eyes sparked angrily and she saw the older woman tense, her expression startled.

'I don't know what you're talking about.'

'Oh, yes, you do, Marina.' Lauranne gave a humourless laugh. 'You set us up five years ago, but do you know something? I don't even care about that any more. All I care about is what you've just done to Zander.' She broke off, not knowing whether to sob or scream, so angry and upset that her breath was coming in pants. 'He wanted this island so badly. Not because it made good business sense but because he made a promise when he was a little boy. A promise to his grandmother, who he adored, made when he was hardly old enough to know what he was promising.'

Emotion choked her and she broke off and covered her mouth with her hand, thinking only of Zander, oblivious to the silence around her.

Kouropoulos was watching her with an odd expression on his face and he pursed his lips thoughtfully. 'You knew that?'

Lauranne lifted damp eyes to his and her hand dropped to her side. 'Yes, I knew that. And I know how hard it was for him to tell me. Zander struggles to trust *anyone* and it's because of women like *you*—' she turned back to Marina, her eyes flashing with anger and contempt '—that he feels that way. You are a *snake.*'

Marina flinched and glanced nervously at her boss but he was still looking at Lauranne.

'You seem astonishingly committed to your role as Zander's defender, young lady.'

'I would do *anything* that helps give Zander a sense of belonging,' she confessed hoarsely, 'and if you're wondering why he can't commit himself to family life then just ask Marina for some clues.' As she realised miserably that she had insulted her host and blown Zander's chances of gaining the island her slim shoulders sagged.

Kouropoulos looked at her thoughtfully. 'You love him that much?'

'Yes. And I'd do anything to make him happy. Absolutely anything.' She turned to Tom with an apologetic shake of her head. 'I know you think I'm crazy—'

He rolled his eyes but then stepped forward and gave her a hug. 'What I think is that you can't help yourself,' he said gruffly, wrapping his arms around her and glaring at Marina. 'And I also think you've done enough. I'll be taking Lauranne home when she's had a chance to pack.'

Lauranne felt tears prick the back of her eyes and blinked them back. She was not going to break down in front of Marina and Kouropoulos. Despite her emotional outburst and her frank confession, she still had some pride.

Now that the deal had fallen through, Zander certainly wouldn't need her any more and she didn't want to hang around any more than she had to or she'd make an utter fool of herself. She might as well go home with Tom.

The fact that Zander had walked off told her everything she needed to know.

He didn't want her.

Kouropoulos turned to Tom, his expression impossible to read. 'There is no flight until this evening. Why don't you come up to the house with us and give Lauranne a chance to gather her things together—' he hesitated slightly '—and do whatever else she needs to do?'

Lauranne looked at him suspiciously. What exactly did he mean by that remark?

There was nothing left to do except go home.

CHAPTER TEN

HAVING packed her things, Lauranne found that she couldn't face joining them in the house so she walked up the path to the white cottage and this time made her way down to the private beach. The path was narrow and steep and she stumbled several times but eventually she made it, and slumped down on the sand, her arms clasped round her legs.

Her emotions were changing so rapidly that she couldn't keep up with them. Anger had turned to misery and then back into anger. How could Zander have just walked out like that? Was he still suspicious of Tom, even after everything she'd told him? She was *so* furious she could hardly think and she didn't know whether to sob out loud or hit something.

And she had no idea where he'd gone. He'd just vanished. Exactly like last time. Just seeing her within a few metres of Tom seemed to fuse his brain cells and she was forced to admit that what she and Zander shared was so fragile that the slightest puff of wind sent it splintering into pieces.

Couldn't he *see* what Marina had done?

Was he *really* that blind?

But then they didn't really have a relationship, she reminded herself, sniffing hard and brushing away a stray tear with the back of her hand.

Zander Volakis wasn't worth crying over.

He was too self-absorbed, too stupidly jealous, too— too—*Greek!*

And she loved him so much it was just *agony*.

At least this time he hadn't exploded, she reflected miserably. He hadn't even tried to throttle Tom. He'd just given her a really funny look and then stalked off into the distance without a word, leaving them staring after him.

Remembering the astonished look on Kouropoulos' face and the smug satisfaction on Marina's, Lauranne gave a groan. There was no way that Zander was going to get his island now.

Marina had once again achieved exactly what she'd set out to achieve.

Havoc.

She struggled to her feet and then froze as a familiar dark drawl came from behind her.

'If you don't stop hugging Farrer when you're almost naked then I won't be held responsible for my actions.'

She whirled round, tears making her eyes bright. She couldn't believe it was him. Standing there. Looking as if he wasn't entirely sure of his reception. 'You stalked out and left me standing there—'

He sucked in a breath and his dark head tilted backwards, strain visible around his eyes. 'Because I was angry— I didn't trust myself—'

She stared at him in an agony of seething frustration. 'Why don't you *ever* use that legendary brain when you're with me? Marina set that up! It was obvious right from the moment that you stupidly told her that we were staying married that she was going to try and mess everything up—you *knew* that—'

'Yes, I knew that.'

She opened her mouth and closed it again, completely deflated by his response. 'Then why were you angry?'

His jaw tightened. 'You were half naked and in his arms. *Again.*'

'I'd been swimming,' she pointed out. 'And of course I hugged him. He's my friend—'

Zander swore violently in Greek, cutting her off. '*Theos mou,* do you think I need reminding of that fact?' He ran a hand through his sleek dark hair, displaying all the signs of maximum discomfort. 'How do you think I feel knowing that he was the one to comfort you when I hurt you so badly—knowing that I drove you into his arms—?'

'Zander—'

'And how do you think I felt today when I saw you in his arms again?' Zander clenched his teeth. 'He came here to pick up the pieces. To take you home. Just as he did last time.'

Lauranne looked at him. 'No,' she said quietly. 'He came because Marina somehow set it up again because she knew it would cause trouble. And it did.' She looked at him miserably. 'I'm *so* sorry about the island.'

His eyes were fixed on her face. 'I don't give a damn about the island.'

For a moment she thought she must have misheard. Of course he cared about the island. Hadn't she given him a new image so that he could buy it? 'But you wanted it so much—'

'I thought I did.' His mouth twisted. 'I discovered that there's something that I want a hell of a lot more.'

Lauranne stared at him, deprived of her powers of speech by a hope so powerful that it threatened to overwhelm her. What was he saying? She didn't dare ask the question, so desperate was she to prolong the fantasy a little longer.

He took a step forwards. 'When I saw Farrer standing there I was so afraid that you'd go with him.'

Finally she found her voice. 'You were afraid?'

'For probably the first time in my life,' he confessed. 'He's always been there for you. He's never let you down, whereas I—' his voice cracked and he ran a hand over his face, struggling with the words '—I have let you down repeatedly. I've treated you very badly, *agape mou,* and I'm more sorry than you'll ever know.'

Lauranne looked at him, stunned. Zander was *apologising?*

Her heart tumbled inside her chest. 'I was at fault too,'

she said softly, stepping closer to him and taking his hands in hers. 'I was the one who made you jealous.'

He gave a wry smile. 'Not a good idea to intentionally make a Greek man jealous.'

'I know that now.'

His smile faded and he stared down into her eyes, a muscle working in his hard jaw. 'All those things Farrer said, about you loving me so much you'd do anything for me—' his voice was hoarse '—were they true?'

Lauranne felt her face heat. It was the first time that her true feelings had been exposed and she suddenly felt shy and unsure.

'Lauranne?' He prompted her gently, his hands sliding over her shoulders and forcing her to look at him. 'Would you do anything for me?'

She nodded, mute, and he let out a long breath.

'That's good to hear.' He pulled her against him and wrapped his arms around her, holding her close. 'Because what I want more than anything is your forgiveness.'

'Forgiveness?'

'For hurting you so badly.' His arms tightened. 'For not trusting you. And then for crashing back into your life and blackmailing you.'

She pulled away slightly and smiled up at him. 'I'm glad you blackmailed me or we'd never be here now. We'd be divorced.'

He shook his head and framed her face with his hands. 'I would *never* have given you a divorce.'

Finally Lauranne summoned the courage to ask the question that she'd been longing to ask.

'Why, Zander?' Her voice faltered slightly. 'Why wouldn't you have given me a divorce?'

A strange expression crossed his handsome face. 'Because I love you.' He said the words softly, as if he was trying them out, and then he smiled and said them again. 'I love you. And I've *never* said those words to anyone before.'

Lauranne stared at him, the tension in her body holding her rigid. 'You really love me? You're sure?'

Please, oh, please—

'Very sure. I think I've always loved you,' he admitted, a wry smile on his face, 'but I didn't recognise it. Or maybe I was too stubborn to recognise it. Five years ago I was terrified by the effect you had on me. It was another reason I removed you from my life so hastily.'

Was it?

Suddenly she wanted to just smile and smile. 'Why did you bring me to the island?'

'Because there was no way I was letting you out of my sight and I wanted to get you away from Farrer,' he said immediately. 'All my instincts told me that it was a bad business decision, but I was determined to do it anyway.'

She stared at him in fascination, utterly captivated by his uncharacteristically emotional response. 'Why was it a bad business decision?'

'Because you were angry with me and I knew you could blow the whole deal if you'd wanted to.' He gave a rueful smile. 'My lawyer has aged ten years since I announced that I was taking you.'

She smiled. 'The moment you told me about your grandmother there was no way I could have ruined it for you. I wanted you to have the island.'

'I know.' His expression was strained. 'You're a good, generous person and I've treated you very badly.'

She shook her head. 'I was stubborn and stupid. I *never* should have tried to make you jealous.'

He nodded assent. 'But the fact that you could, should have told you something.'

She smiled. 'Apart from the fact that you're Greek?'

'It should have told you that I was in love with you,' he said hoarsely, bending his head to kiss her mouth. 'I can't let you do it, Lauranne. I ought to be generous and tell you that Farrer is right. That I'm a selfish bastard and you're probably better off without me. But I can't do it. I can't be that generous. I won't give you a divorce. You're mine. And I intend to spend the rest of my life making up for hurting you so badly.'

Her heart warmed but she lifted her chin, unable to resist teasing him. 'And what if I want a divorce?'

He shook his head and pulled her close once more. 'You don't.'

'And what makes you so sure of yourself, Mr Volakis?'

'Your reasons for marrying me five years ago.' His arms tightened around her. 'If you were truly after my money, why didn't you ever spend any?'

'Because the only thing I really wanted wasn't for sale.' She hesitated, her eyes soft as she laid bare her heart. 'I wanted you to let me close. I wanted you to let me love you. And I wanted you to love me back.'

'I did. And if I wasn't so stubborn, I might have realised it earlier,' he confessed with a groan. 'If you hadn't kissed Farrer to make me jealous, if you'd flung accusations at me instead of trying to beat me at my own game, we might never have reached the point we did. But I know now that I should have trusted you.'

'You're forgetting Marina,' Lauranne pointed out. 'She still would have found a way to break us up.'

He grimaced. 'But I would have listened to you if I hadn't been so enraged with jealousy.'

'You fired me on the spot.'

He groaned and ran a hand over his face. 'Don't remind me. All I can say in my defence is that I was so shattered by the effect you had on me that I wanted to get you out of my life. You were the first woman who had ever made me believe in love and I was afraid of it.'

She reached up and touched his cheek with her fingers, her expression soft. 'Your father was unlucky, Zander.'

'I know.' His eyes burned into hers. 'Whereas I'm extremely lucky, *agape mou*—'

'So what happens now?' Her eyes were sparkling as she wrapped her arms around his neck.

His eyes dropped to her mouth, his expression uncertain. 'How would you feel about having full and personal responsibility for my public image for the rest of our lives?'

Wanting to tease him just a little longer, she lifted an eyebrow. 'You're employing me full time?'

He gave a frustrated groan and lowered his mouth to hers. 'I'm asking you to stay married to me,' he murmured against her lips, 'for ever. I want you. By my side. As my wife.'

She kissed him back, deeply touched by his uncharacteristically emotional words. 'Yes,' she breathed, 'yes, yes—'

He dragged his mouth away from hers long enough to mutter, 'Farrer will kill me—' and then kissed her again long and deep until she clutched at his shirt, breathless and dizzy.

'I think he's washed his hands of me,' she confessed, 'and he definitely thinks I have very bad taste in men.'

Zander gave an unsteady laugh. 'You probably do. Why else would you want to stay married to me? Apart from the great sex and the credit card without a limit?'

She grinned. 'I probably shouldn't have said that.'

'No. I deserved it. I gave you no reason to think the relationship was anything other than physical even though the evidence to the contrary was staring us both in the face. I didn't recognise love then.' He kissed her again. 'But I do now. And I'm going to be uttering words of love until I lose my voice.'

Utterly enchanted by this new, demonstrative Zander, Lauranne pulled away from him wanting to hear more. 'When did you finally realise you loved me?'

'It crept up on me,' he confessed, 'but I had a fairly strong inkling when I found myself telling you all sorts of personal details that I never tell anyone and then being unable to leave you alone even for one moment. It may have escaped your notice but even when I was using the laptop I could have reached out and touched you.'

She smiled. It *hadn't* escaped her notice.

'You are a major distraction,' he said ruefully, 'and I think with you by my side the business may well crash and burn. Telling Kouropoulos that we were staying married was a wild impulse that startled me as much as it did you. I think subconsciously I was asking you in public because I was afraid that if I did it in private you might refuse me.'

'I didn't think you meant it.' Lauranne tipped her head on one side, her smile teasing. 'So why did you walk away earlier?'

'Because I didn't trust myself around Tom,' he confessed ruefully. 'And because I thought you might want to take his advice and go with him.'

'But you came back for me—'

He gave a helpless shrug. 'I decided that I'm not very good at self-sacrifice,' he confessed. 'You're mine. I didn't intend to give you up without a fight.'

'If you'd stayed to fight then maybe Kouropoulos would have agreed to sell you the island,' she said regretfully and a deep voice interrupted them both.

'I would indeed.'

They both turned to find Theo Kouropoulos watching them with benign amusement.

'So is this marriage fake or real?'

Zander looked at Lauranne and she smiled, everything in her heart shining from her eyes. 'It's real. Very real.'

Zander pulled her back to him with a groan of all-male satisfaction, dropping a fleeting kiss on her mouth.

Kouropoulos gave a grunt of approval. 'In that case the island is yours.'

Lauranne gave a gasp of astonishment and a delighted smile spread over her face. 'Really?'

'Really.' He looked at Zander, a keen expression in his eyes. 'I knew about your promise to your grandmother and I knew that you weren't in a position to fulfil it for many years while you were building up the business so I, too, made a promise. I promised your father before he died that I would sell it to no one but you.'

Zander looked stunned. 'You spoke to my father about it?' His voice was hoarse and Kouropoulos shrugged.

'He felt very bad about what had happened and he wanted to make sure that one day the island would be restored to its rightful owner. He had faith in you. He knew you'd rescue his business and build it into something to be proud of.'

Zander closed his eyes briefly. 'All these years you've refused to sell—'

'Because I made a promise to your father.' Kouropoulos nodded, a satisfied expression on his face. 'I was waiting for you to come to me. You took your time.'

'Because you'd always refused to sell. But I kept an eye on the business and I could see that you were struggling. I was waiting for you to finally admit that you needed help.' Zander stared at him. 'And all this stuff about my image—'

'Your father felt extraordinarily guilty that he'd ruined your trust in women. He wanted to see you in a loving relationship.' Kouropoulos smiled. 'Call me an interfering old man, but I thought I'd try a bit of manipulation and, by some sort of miracle and a whole lot of luck, it worked. If I needed evidence that the two of you really love each other, I just had it. The island is yours, Volakis. Welcome home, Zander.'

And with that he turned and walked back up the beach without a backward glance, leaving them alone together.

For several minutes Zander didn't speak and Lauranne knew that he was battling with his emotions. So was she.

'What a lovely man.' Her voice was choked and Zander nodded, his expression thoughtful.

'He almost allowed himself to get into financial difficulties and I could never understand why.'

'Your father wanted to make it up to you,' she said softly and he nodded, his voice rough with emotion.

'I know that now.'

'I'm so pleased.' She lifted a hand and touched his face. 'So what will you do with the island?'

He turned and smiled down at her, everything he felt reflected in his eyes. 'Exactly what I told Kouropoulos. I want it for my wife and family. We're going to make babies, *agape mou,* and this is going to be their home.'

Exactly a year later Tom was a guest at a housewarming party on Blue Cove Island.

'House?' he grumbled, staring at the beautiful whitewashed villa in amazement. 'You call that a *house?* It's a mansion.'

'It's my home,' Lauranne said softly, still unable to believe that she actually lived in this beautiful place.

Builders and decorators had worked overtime to complete the villa so that the couple could move in as soon as possible.

'So he's treating you OK, then,' Tom said dryly and Lauranne glanced across to where Zander stood, her eyes misty with love.

'Better than OK,' she said softly. 'He's wonderful.'

Tom gave a grunt. 'He finally seems to be behaving himself, I'll give you that. Being with you seems to have mellowed him. He lets me talk to you now without setting the dogs on me.'

'But not for too long.' Lauranne chuckled. 'He's coming over now.'

Tom tensed but Zander smiled and extended a hand, the perfect host.

The two men chatted together about business and the

building of the villa and then Tom made his excuses and backed away, leaving the two of them together.

Lauranne looked at Zander and slid her hand in his. 'Thank you for inviting him,' she said softly, standing on tiptoe to kiss his cheek. 'Your self-restraint is improving daily.'

'Just as long as you keep the physical stuff to a minimum,' Zander growled, stooping to kiss her lips. 'Underneath my civilised exterior, I'm still Greek. Remember that.'

'Am I really likely to forget?' Lauranne smiled up at him and then looked at their new home thoughtfully. 'How many bedrooms did we decide on in the end?'

Zander shot her an incredulous look, obviously recalling the endless discussions with the team of architects. 'If that is a serious question—'

She kept her expression innocent, deriving the maximum enjoyment from teasing him. 'It's just that we're going to be needing another one soon.'

'We are?' He looked at her blankly and she smiled.

'For a very intelligent man you can be extremely slow sometimes,' she said softly, taking his hand and placing it low on her abdomen. 'We're having a baby.'

He stilled. 'A *baby?*'

She nodded, smiling at the stunned expression on his face. 'And it's going to be born here on the island, just as your grandmother was.' She looked at him anxiously, her eyes full of love. 'Are you pleased?'

'Pleased?' He looked at her and then grinned, staggeringly handsome and endearingly smug about his latest achievement. 'Of course I'm pleased.'

He scooped her into his arms, and strode towards the beach, totally ignoring the curious looks they were receiving from the other guests.

'Zander—' Lauranne closed her eyes in embarrassment '—you're behaving like a caveman.'

Zander smiled. 'I'm Greek, remember? Behaving like a caveman is what I do best.'

She peeped at him flirtatiously. 'Actually I can think of something that you probably do better—'

He set her down in the sand, away from the crowds of people they'd invited to their new home.

'Can you now?' His voice was husky and unbelievably sexy as he bent his head to kiss her. 'Care to show me?'

'With pleasure,' she whispered, standing on tiptoe to receive his kiss. 'With pleasure.'

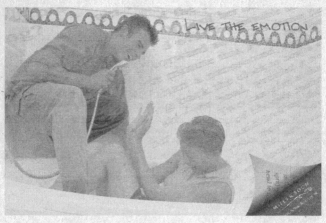

Your opinion is important to us!

Please take a few moments to share your thoughts with us about Mills & Boon® and Silhouette® books. Your comments will ensure that we continue to deliver books you love to read.

To thank you for your input, everyone who replies will be entered into a prize draw to win a year's supply of their favourite series books*.

1. There are several different series under the Mills & Boon and Silhouette brands. Please tick the box that most accurately represents your reading habit for each series.

Series	Currently Read (have read within last three months)	Used to Read (but do not read currently)	Do Not Read
Mills & Boon			
Modern Romance™	❏	❏	❏
Sensual Romance™	❏	❏	❏
Blaze™	❏	❏	❏
Tender Romance™	❏	❏	❏
Medical Romance™	❏	❏	❏
Historical Romance™	❏	❏	❏
Silhouette			
Special Edition™	❏	❏	❏
Superromance™	❏	❏	❏
Desire™	❏	❏	❏
Sensation™	❏	❏	❏
Intrigue™	❏	❏	❏

2. Where did you buy this book?

From a supermarket ❏ Through our Reader Service™ ❏
From a bookshop ❏ If so please give us your Club Subscription no.
On the Internet ❏

Other _____ _____ / _____

3. Please indicate by number which were the 3 most important factors that made you buy this book. (1 = most important).

The picture on the cover	___	I enjoy this series	___
The author	___	The price	___
The title	___	I borrowed/was given this book	___
The description on the back cover	___	Part of a mini-series	___

Other _____

4. How many Mills & Boon and /or Silhouette books do you buy at one time?

I buy ___ books at one time ❏
I rarely buy a book (less than once a year) ❏

5. How often do you shop for any Mills & Boon and/or Silhouette books?

One or more times a month ❏ A few times per year ❏
Once every 2-3 months ❏ Never ❏

6. How long have you been reading Mills & Boon® and/or Silhouette®?
_____ years

7. What other types of book do you enjoy reading?

Family sagas eg. Maeve Binchy ❑
Classics eg. Jane Austen ❑
Historical sagas eg. Josephine Cox ❑
Crime/Thrillers eg. John Grisham ❑
Romance eg. Danielle Steel ❑
Science Fiction/Fantasy eg. JRR Tolkien ❑
Contemporary Women's fiction eg. Marian Keyes ❑

8. Do you agree with the following statements about Mills & Boon? Please tick the appropriate boxes.

	Strongly agree	Tend to agree	Neither agree nor disagree	Tend to disagree	Strongly disagree
Mills & Boon offers great value for money.	❑	❑	❑	❑	❑
With Mills & Boon I can always find the right type of story to suit my mood.	❑	❑	❑	❑	❑
I read Mills & Boon books because they offer me an entertaining escape from everyday life.	❑	❑	❑	❑	❑
Mills & Boon stories have improved or stayed the same standard over the time I have been reading them.	❑	❑	❑	❑	❑

9. Which age bracket do you belong to? Your answers will remain confidential.

❑ 16-24   ❑ 25-34   ❑ 35-49   ❑ 50-64   ❑ 65+

THANK YOU for taking the time to tell us what you think! If you would like to be entered into the **FREE prize draw** to win a year's supply of your favourite series books, please enter your name and address below.

Name: _____

Address: _____

_____

Post Code: _____ Tel: _____

Please send your completed questionnaire to the address below:

READER SURVEY, PO Box 676, Richmond, Surrey, TW9 1WU.

* Prize is equivalent to 4 books a month, for twelve months, for your chosen series. No purchase necessary. To obtain a questionnaire and entry form, please write to the address above. Closing date 31st December 2004. Draw date no later than 15th January 2005. Full set of rules available upon request. Open to all residents of the UK and Eire, aged 18 years and over.

As a result of this application, you may receive offers from Harlequin Mills & Boon Ltd. If you do not wish to share in this opportunity please write to the data manager at the address shown above.
® and ™ are trademarks owned and used by the owner and/or its licensee.

FREE!
4 Books
and a surprise gift!

We would like to take this opportunity to thank you for reading this Mills & Boon® book by offering you the chance to take FOUR more specially selected titles from the Modern Romance™ series absolutely FREE! We're also making this offer to introduce you to the benefits of the Reader Service™—

- ★ **FREE home delivery**
- ★ **FREE gifts and competitions**
- ★ **FREE monthly Newsletter**
- ★ **Exclusive Reader Service offers**
- ★ **Books available before they're in the shops**

Accepting these FREE books and gift places you under no obligation to buy, you may cancel at any time, even after receiving your free shipment. Simply complete your details below and return the entire page to the address below. You don't even need a stamp!

YES! Please send me 4 free Modern Romance books and a surprise gift. I understand that unless you hear from me, I will receive 6 superb new titles every month for just £2.69 each, postage and packing free. I am under no obligation to purchase any books and may cancel my subscription at any time. The free books and gift will be mine to keep in any case.

P4ZEF

Ms/Mrs/Miss/Mr ....Initials...........................
BLOCK CAPITALS PLEASE

Surname ....

Address..

....

....Postcode ....

Send this whole page to:
UK: FREEPOST CN81, Croydon, CR9 3WZ